Collision

ANTHONY WALL

Collision

DRAGON
GRAFTON BOOKS
A Division of the Collins Publishing Group

LONDON GLASGOW
TORONTO SYDNEY AUCKLAND

Dragon
Grafton Books
A Division of the Collins Publishing Group
8 Grafton Street, London W1X 3LA

Published by Dragon Books 1986

First published by Granada Publishing
in hardback 1985

ISBN 0-583-30759-0

Printed and bound in Great Britain by
Collins, Glasgow

Set in Times

For my young friend
Spencer, whose
enthusiasm
helped fuel mine

Acknowledgements

I am indebted to my wife Barbara for her unfailing support during the writing of this book; to Jill Campbell Mackay for planting the seeds of an idea; to Geoff Cowan and Ted Cowan for their expert advice; to Derek Hall for cheering me on at every stage.

My research for *Collision* was greatly aided by staff of the following bodies: Lloyd's Register of Shipping, the Admiralty, the Department of Trade, British Petroleum, Shell International, the Cunard Steam-Ship Company, Dover Coastguard, Southampton Dock Board, the Port of London Authority, the National Maritime Museum, the Royal Society for the Prevention of Cruelty to Animals, the Royal Society for the Protection of Birds, and the Embassy of the State of Kuwait.

Finally, I must acknowledge the importance of Noel Mostart's excellent book, *Supership*, as a source of reference.

Note:

The background details of *Collision* are as accurate and authentic as I can make them. But, here and there, I have 'played' with the facts for the sake of telling a dramatic story. All the places mentioned are real, with the exception of Southead and Belton.

CHAPTER ONE

The Rogue

Gary groaned. What a rotten day! Pressing his nose against the window, he peered out at a blank, grey wall. Fog. He could hear ships' horns hooting, like the voices of lost animals. The big ships mooed and the smaller ones bleated as they crept through the English Channel, wrapped in clammy cloud.

Disappointment was written all over Gary's face when he turned his back on the gloomy view. He'd been looking forward to today for ages. It wasn't often he had the chance to join his father watching ships from the traffic control room at Southead, Britain's busiest port.

'Cheer up, lad.' Commander Izzard grinned and ruffled the thirteen-year-old's mop of black hair. 'The weather may clear. Anyway, there's still plenty to see and do here.'

'Okay, Dad.' Gary tried to appear bright. He glanced around the control room. An officer sitting before a radar screen caught his eye and winked. Gary wandered over and stood beside the man, a ruddy-cheeked young lieutenant named Mitchell. Together they stared at the lines of luminous green dots on the screen.

'Ships,' explained Mitchell. 'Hundreds of 'em. The Channel is the most crowded stretch of sea in the world. It's always rush-hour. Our job is to keep the traffic flowing smoothly and to catch any "road hogs". You'd be surprised how many there are.'

'A bit like being a policeman,' said Gary.

'Yes,' agreed the lieutenant. 'The sea has its own

highway code. Vessels must keep to the right and stay in the correct lane. But quite a few don't. They tear along in the wrong lane against the oncoming traffic – and sometimes there's a terrible accident. We call those ships Rogues.'

Gary frowned. 'But why do they do it, these Rogues?'

Mitchell shrugged. 'Maybe because the captains want to save time, or because they're bad seamen and couldn't care less about the rules. Who can say? All I know is, Rogues are a dangerous menace. And the people in charge of them ought to be locked up . . .'

The lieutenant fell silent. Gary studied the patterns on the radar screen for a moment longer, then padded towards the window. He stuck his nose to the cold glass again. The fog seemed even thicker. Some summer! Why couldn't it have been like the last time he visited his father at work? Gary remembered that sunny June day . . .

A black-and-white launch had frisked up to the harbour quay. Ropes were thrown, and in an instant the craft was tethered. Gary jumped aboard. Soon the trim little launch was swaggering through the estuary to a new destination – Southead traffic control room – six miles away. Eagerly, he had scanned the changing scene. Ships everywhere. All shapes and sizes. Lean liners, fat freighters, vessels from the seven seas –

'Gary . . . Gary . . . *Gary*!' Commander Izzard gently shook his son's shoulder. 'Day-dreaming again?' Gary blinked, saw the window and the swirling fog beyond. 'Sorry, Dad. I was just thinking of the last time I was here.'

He walked with his father across the traffic control room. Lieutenant Mitchell still sat at the radar screen.

'Spotted any Rogues?' asked Gary, rather cheekily.

'No, and there'd better not be any!' Mitchell sounded angry. Gary was surprised. Then Commander Izzard spoke: 'Rogues aren't funny, son. Sink other ships and drown sailors, that's what Rogues can do.'

Gary imagined a car driver suddenly seeing another car speeding towards him on the wrong side of the road. Meeting a Rogue at sea must be a bit like that – only cars could swerve more easily than ships. In fog, it would be even worse . . .

His father noticed Gary's worried expression. 'Come on, m'lad, let's do something useful. You can help me check the list of vessels arriving and departing today.'

They went to Commander Izzard's desk. Gary glanced at his father, who gazed back kindly. The two were very much alike – dark haired and dark eyed with squarish, friendly faces. At forty-five, Commander David Izzard had more than earned his senior rank. He was popular in the control room, despite being a stickler for discipline and somewhat stiff and starchy when on duty. Gary admired him greatly, even if he *was* a bit old fashioned. The Commander thought a lot of his son, too. Although small for his age, Gary was wiry and athletic. He was also quick witted. But what his father liked best was the boy's honesty.

'Right, down to work,' Commander Izzard said briskly. Gary smiled to himself. He loved his mother, and even his bossy older sister and whiny kid brother, but he'd rather be with his father than anyone else in the world.

Gary sang out the names of the ships . . . *Liberty, Rhine Maiden, Olympus* . . . from a list, while his father stuck coloured pins into a chart. At least half the vessels had been delayed by the weather.

'Well, that's that,' said the Commander when they'd finished. Gary leant forward in his chair, feeling slightly restless. 'Wish we could see a supertanker, Dad, one of those 500,000 tonners.'

Commander Izzard snorted. 'Huh, supertankers! Dirty, ugly, unsafe monsters. Too big to steer properly. Always getting wrecked, spilling their oil, polluting the sea and the land. Supertankers – you can keep 'em.'

'Yes. But, Dad . . .'

'Son, if you'd seen the old passenger liner *Queen Elizabeth*, you wouldn't want to waste time looking at tankers. What a beauty she was! Real royalty.'

Gary sat back, knowing that his father had launched a favourite subject.

'Used to glide into Southead as though she owned the ocean,' continued the Commander. 'A graceful giant of 84,000 tons, biggest and best liner ever built. The *Queen* would be escorted to her berth by nine tugs, all curtsying like ladies-in-waiting. Don't talk to me about supertankers!'

Gary grinned. 'All right, Dad. I won't.' Then he added, stubbornly: 'I'd still like to see one, though. Fat chance today.'

There was a long silence. The Commander started to drum his fingers, a sure sign something was wrong. But what? Gary's father could be moody occasionally. The silence grew heavier. Now Commander Izzard was scowling.

A little nervously, Gary said: 'Er . . . Dad, why are you angry? Is it my fault?'

His father replied, quite quietly. 'No, it's not your fault. Supertankers make me edgy, that's all. Every time one comes to the oil refinery out there,' he pointed towards the fog-curtained window, 'I grit my teeth. What if a tanker collided with another vessel, say a liner? The explosion could blow them both sky high – and cause havoc in the port. Death, destruction . . . a nightmare!'

Gary pondered for a moment. 'Surely Southead wouldn't let that happen.'

'We take precautions, son. Plenty. Southead *should* be safe. But supertankers are such clumsy great brutes and the captains and crews aren't always good seamen. There've been so many accidents around the world . . .'

Father and son sat thinking. Suddenly, Commander Izzard stood up and stretched. His natural cheerfulness was beginning to bob to the surface. 'Enough of this gloom, Gary. You're here to enjoy yourself.'

Soon Gary was studying a book of ships' silhouettes, a useful guide in vessel identification. He broke off to eat the ham and tomato sandwiches his mother had packed for him that morning. Afterwards, he put on a pair of earphones and listened to radio messages from the sea traffic. Two hours flew by unnoticed.

Then Gary decided to look again at the radar screen. It was three minutes past three. He would remember that time, checked on his brand new watch, for years to come. Lieutenant Mitchell had gone to fetch a cup of coffee, so Gary took a seat in front of the screen. What he saw made him call out.

'Dad!'

Commander Izzard hurried over.

'I may be wrong,' said Gary, 'but isn't that a . . . ?'

'Rogue!' confirmed the Commander, eyes blazing. 'Going at a helluva lick. In this weather! Captain's a madman!'

Gary goggled. His father's face was grim, almost frightening.

'Mitchell!' barked Commander Izzard to the returning lieutenant. 'Tell emergency services to stand by – fire, hospital, air and sea rescue. I'll alert all ships in the area. Hope to blazes we can divert that damned Rogue before it's too late!'

Gary started to speak. 'Not now, son,' said the Commander. 'This could be nasty, very nasty indeed . . .'

CHAPTER TWO

Terror in the fog

The supertanker *Olympus* 'felt' its way forward through dense fog, using radar as a blind man uses his stick. Twelve miles to Southead. Another voyage nearly over. The voyage had begun six weeks earlier in sweltering heat and dazzling light when *Olympus* set out from the Persian Gulf with 220,000 tons of crude oil for Britain. Oil that would be refined; transformed into petrol, paraffin, plastics, gas, wax, detergents and many more products.

On the bridge of the supertanker, Captain Duncan Farrar paced restlessly. And it wasn't only the fog that made him uneasy. This had been an unlucky trip – fatal for one poor sailor. Farrar winced at the memory of that sudden, unexpected death.

Olympus had been cruising through a clear blue sea under a clear blue sky. Porpoises played in the ship's bow wave, while flying fish flashed silver arcs across the frothy wake trailing astern. A perfect day. Then, without warning, a freak gale blew up. The whirling wind snatched a crew member off the deck and hurled him overboard. As soon as Farrar heard what had happened, he ordered *Olympus* to turn, a manoeuvre that would take half a mile. To come to a complete halt, the heavy supertanker would need two and a half miles. And anchors dropped to stop the huge vessel would simply snap their cables or rip the deck off like the lid of a sardine tin. Through binoculars, Farrar anxiously watched the sailor's bobbing head in the distance. At least he could swim. *Olympus* would save him. But then tragedy struck. Farrar saw the man's face twist in horror and panic, saw a scream that couldn't be heard. When *Olympus* arrived on the scene, the sailor's corpse was floating peacefully – surrounded by sea snakes. Yellow-bellied sea snakes, deadlier than the king cobra. The ship's crew looked on, stunned. Even sharks were less loathed than these repulsive reptiles which, so reports said, had once been sighted wriggling in a convoy ten feet wide and sixty miles long. Several seamen were sick. The sailor's body was brought aboard. Later, Farrar entered the incident in the ship's log and wrote to the man's relatives. Perhaps the Moslem crew members would mention their lost shipmate when they knelt on their prayer mats and bowed towards Mecca, as they did every day.

Captain Farrar rubbed his forehead, pushing the unhappy memory from his mind, and tried to concentrate on the present. Eleven miles to Southead. *Olympus* sounded its booming fog horn.

'Everything okay, number one?' asked Farrar.

'Yes, thank you, sir,' said the first officer.

Of course everything was okay! Farrar knew there was no need for him to be on the bridge now. His officers could handle the ship as well as he could. So why was he worried? Why was he haunted by the feeling that this voyage still had a shock in store? Was some terror waiting for them behind the grey murk?

Must be getting old, he thought. It's the trip that's made me jumpy. He glanced around at the screens, dials, buttons and switches – the bridge looked like a creation from science-fiction.

Ten miles to Southead.

'Two degrees starboard,' ordered the first officer.

'Aye, aye, sir.' A rating at the wheel adjusted

course, while the officer phoned the engine room 150 feet below with instructions to keep the ship's speed at Slow Ahead.

Farrar stared blankly towards the bow, quarter of a mile away. Even on a clear day, he needed a telescope to see details at that distance. So big was the vessel that sailors sometimes rode bicycles across the acres of red-painted deck to save time, and all officers carried walkie-talkie radios. Yet the 250,000-ton *Olympus* was only medium-sized for a super-tanker.

Sighing, Farrar wondered how he had ever come to command such a monstrosity. He loved ships. But who could love a supertanker, which didn't rise and fall with the waves but barged through them like a floating pier? The officers and crew called *Olympus* 'it', never 'she'.

Nine miles to Southead. Nearly in port, thought Captain Farrar. And the fog seems to be lifting a little. Surely nothing else can go wrong now. But a nagging doubt remained.

Eight miles to Southead.

A brief survey of the bridge told Farrar that the first officer had everything under control. The captain returned to his thoughts. What a life! Haven't set foot on dry land for a year. *Olympus* never stopped working. No sooner was the oil cargo loaded or unloaded than the supertanker set off again to earn more money for its rich owners. Sometimes the ship's destination would be changed in mid-voyage because demand for oil was greater in one country than another, and the price would be higher. To avoid costly delays, supplies and mail were ferried aboard by helicopter or launch at the Cape of Good Hope.

Money – that's all anybody seems to care about

these days, mused Farrar. But what about safety? Supertankers were badly designed, and often broke down. Several times, *Olympus* had drifted helplessly towards jagged rocks that could have ripped its hull and spilt the oil. Fortunately, the ship's engineer had managed to re-start the engines on each occasion. But one day, they wouldn't be so lucky. *Olympus* – 250,000 tons of trouble with a lifespan of only fifteen years, not like a *real* ship which could go on giving good service for up to eighty years!

Seven miles to Southead. The fog definitely looked thinner. Farrar's spirits rose. Soon be there. He started to hum to himself. *Olympus* would reach the refinery without harm. What a fool I was, worrying about nothing! Like a kid, frightened of spooks. He was glad he hadn't mentioned his fears to the first officer. The closer they drew to port, the more relaxed Farrar became.

Six miles to Southead.

The first officer shot a glance at his superior. 'Feeling more cheerful, sir?'

'Yes, number one. I'm looking forward to going home on leave for a couple of months. See the wife, children – both grown up – and grandchildren. Do some gardening, pop down to the local pub. You must visit us in Scotland on your next leave.'

'Thank you, sir. By the way, do you know who'll be taking over from you at Southead?'

'Nope. But he's very welcome, whoever he is!'

Farrar sat down in the Captain's Chair. The tension at the back of his neck had eased. In a year or two, he'd retire. No more worries with supertankers. And this trip was almost finished. Nothing to fear now . . .

'Captain Farrar, sir.' The radio operator saluted smartly. 'Urgent message from Southead traffic control room.'

'Well, what is it?' Farrar felt the tension creeping into his neck again.

'Can't make it all out, sir. There's interference on our radio. But I did hear the word "Rogue".'

'Keep at it, man. Let me know the moment you make clear contact with Southead.'

Farrar began pacing the bridge. Maybe the radio operator had been mistaken. Or maybe the Rogue was in another part of the Channel. But Farrar couldn't convince himself.

Five miles to Southead.

Olympus blew a long blast on its fog horn.

Captain Farrar chewed his lip and continued pacing.

The radio operator came back. 'Message complete, sir. There's a Rogue. Steaming at full speed. In our area . . .'

Farrar flinched. 'Number one, tell the engine room to reduce revs – Dead Slow. And watch that ruddy radar screen!'

At Southead traffic control room, Gary was watching the radar screen. Two green dots moved towards each other as if pulled by magnets. Commander Izzard kept broadcasting his warning. Lieutenant Mitchell had alerted rescue services. Gary found it hard to breathe.

On the bridge of *Olympus*, the first officer exclaimed: 'Got the swine, sir! There.' He jabbed the screen with a finger.

The Rogue was close, very close. Farrar grabbed a short-range VHF radio and tried to contact the vessel. No reply. He tried again and again, without success.

The seconds ticked by. Four and a half miles to Southead. Then Captain Farrar went white. Out of the fog loomed a ship. A big ship. Too late to steer clear. Vainly, he raised his arms. 'Get away! Get away!' But the Rogue charged closer. Pictures of his family flashed through his head. 'Send an SOS!' he shouted at the radio operator. The Rogue was almost on top of them.

To his surprise, Farrar felt quite calm. 'We've had it,' he murmured. 'We've had it.'

CHAPTER THREE

Abandon ship!

The two green dots danced side by side, then came together. Oh, no! Gary gaped at the radar screen. In his mind, he heard the crash and crunch of steel as the ships collided. He imagined the sea surging through huge ragged holes in their hulls. And what of the crews . . . ?

Commander Izzard licked his dry lips and listened sadly to the SOS from *Olympus*. There was nothing he could do – it was up to the rescue teams now.

'No explosion, sir,' commented Lieutenant Mitchell.

'Not so far,' the Commander said, pessimistically. 'But one spark can change that. It's a miracle the tanker didn't blow up on impact. Damned Rogue!'

A muffled roar reached them. Gary ran to the window. Through the fog, slowly shredding in a fresh breeze, he saw a flotilla of rescue vessels leaving port. He counted . . . twenty or more. Tugs, hovercraft, cruisers, launches, fire-fighting and hospital ships. Forming a giant V, they lunged into the thumping grey waves of the English Channel. Above and ahead of the arrowing flotilla, three helicopters hovered as if leading an attack.

Gary watched, wide-eyed. Then he left the window, passing an officer who was broadcasting news of the collision to all nearby ships, and sidled up to his father. Impatiently, he fidgeted until Commander Izzard noticed him.

'Dad, can I – ?'

'Sorry, son. No chance.' The Commander read Gary like a book.

'But why not?'

'Because I say so. You can't go out to the wrecks, Gary. First, it's dangerous – *Olympus* might still explode. Second, the rescuers are already on their way and, besides, they wouldn't want you getting under their feet. Third, your mother – '

Lieutenant Mitchell interrupted. 'Excuse me, sir. But there is a survey ship – *Trident* – setting off in a couple of minutes. Gary would be perfectly safe on board, if they'd take him.'

Gary grinned at the lieutenant and turned to his father with an appealing look.

Commander Izzard raised his eyebrows, glared at Mitchell and muttered: 'Hmm, seems I'm outnumbered. All right, Lieutenant,' he added. 'As it's your bright idea, you can call *Trident* to ask for permission. But I don't suppose they'll agree.'

Gary hopped up and down while Mitchell spoke into the radio-telephone. He stopped talking, listened, then gave the boy a wink. Gary understood. His eyes sparkled. 'Great!'

'Okay, son,' said the Commander. 'You win. But don't tell your mother – she'd skin me alive if she knew. And mind you obey orders on the ship.'

Gary felt like hugging his father, but suddenly became shy in front of the other men. So he just said: 'Thanks a million, Dad.' Slipping on his anorak, he hurried downstairs. *Trident* was nudging the jetty.

'Welcome aboard, young feller.' The captain's handshake almost hurt. 'Glad to meet Commander Izzard's boy. Fine man, your father.'

Gary beamed.

Then the captain's face grew serious. 'I must warn you, though, we may see some pretty unpleasant things on this trip. Sure you want to come?'

Gary, equally solemn, nodded and thought again of the shipwrecked sailors.

'Very well,' said the captain.

Seconds later, *Trident* cast off her moorings and nosed towards the open sea. A sudden shaft of sunlight found its way through the tattered fog. The vast silver domes of the oil refinery gleamed coldly in the distance, giving Gary a slightly creepy feeling. *Trident* increased speed and began to rise and fall. They were in the Channel at last.

An officer joined the captain on the bridge. 'Rotten business, eh, sir? I'd like to get my hands on the master of that Rogue. Ruddy lunatic! Blindly belting along. And of all the ships to hit . . . a supertanker!'

The captain grunted his agreement. '*Olympus* could have gone off like a bomb and killed everyone on both vessels. But it's the oil that worries me.'

'Pollution, you mean, sir.'

'Right. More than 200,000 tons of crude oil gushing into the sea. A disaster. Cause a fantastic amount of damage. Wipe out fish and birds, ruin beaches. I hate to think of it.'

'Maybe the oil tanks weren't holed, sir.'

'Maybe. We'll know soon enough. But if there are blokes in the water and they swallow oil, they're gonners. That brown muck rots your guts.'

The two men suddenly noticed Gary listening. 'Want to see over *Trident*?' said the officer. 'Might be able to rustle up some grub, too.' Gary smiled, less broadly than before, and followed the man below.

Like every survey ship, *Trident* was packed with equipment for studying the sea-bed. This information, on the depth of the water and the position of navigational hazards such as wrecks, went into Admiralty Charts – a vital aid to mariners. Gary tried to pay attention as the officer explained echo-sounders and other electronic marvels, but his thoughts kept wandering. Explosions, oil, dying sailors . . . Gary imagined the Rogue's master with a devil's face. Why had the senseless collision occurred?

'Grub up.' A rating handed Gary two ham rolls on a plate and a glass of lemonade. The boy mumbled 'Thanks', without really looking.

At Southead traffic control room, life was returning to normal. Lieutenant Mitchell and his fellow officers had resumed routine duties, ensuring that the sea traffic flowed smoothly. But Commander Izzard couldn't settle down. Anxiety fluttered in his stomach. Shouldn't have let Gary go. He's only a lad. Too young for ugly sights, though he's got to learn sooner or later . . .

Mitchell stepped forward. 'Call for you, sir. It's Gary.'

The Commander wasted no time in picking up the phone.

'How are you doing, son? Any problems?'

'I'm fine, Dad. Just wanted to talk to you.'

'Where are you?'

'Oh, about two miles from the wrecks. Still can't see much in this fog. Dad, they say there could be lots of pollution. Is that right?'

'Afraid so, but perhaps it can be stopped. Now you understand why I'm not nuts about supertankers.'

'Yes. But the Rogue's worse – almost, well, evil . . .'

'I know what you mean, Gary. Gives *me* the creeps, too. Anyway, you should be back in three or four hours. Tell me all about it then. Sure you're okay?'

'Course I am, Dad. Bye.'

Commander Izzard put down the phone. The corners of his mouth lifted 'Not much wrong with you, son,' he murmured.

A tug hooted. *Trident*'s diesel engines drummed powerfully – she was catching up the flotilla.

By now, a helicopter hung hawk-like over the collision area. Strangely, the fog had dispersed around the wrecked ships, leaving a cloudless ring. Peering down, the pilot was reminded of a forest clearing. In the circle, spotlighted by the sun, *Olympus* was sinking fast. Oil oozed from the torn hull like blood from a wounded whale. Not far away, the upraised stern of a vessel – another tanker? – slid beneath the waves. Near where the Rogue had vanished, men rowed hard in bobbing lifeboats. Odd, thought the pilot. Were they ignoring the five or six figures struggling in the brown-stained water by *Olympus*, or was it just his imagination? But the question didn't linger in his mind. There was so much happening at once. He had work to do, and the clock was against him. What a mess . . . ! He guided the helicopter lower. A second airman prepared the rescue line to fish men out of the sea.

Reports from the pilot reached the approaching flotilla, only half a mile behind. *Trident*'s captain grimaced. Well, at least the supertanker wouldn't blow up now, he thought. But that leaking oil! Those sailors in the water! Had they swallowed the muck? Would they be sucked under when *Olympus* sank? Why hadn't they been rescued yet?

Standing beside him on the bridge, Gary and the officer could almost hear the captain thinking. The officer shook his head. 'I can still hardly believe it, sir. This collision should never have happened. Must've been absolute hell . . .'

Yes, the collision had been hell – as Duncan Farrar, master of *Olympus*, would later testify. When the Rogue had burst through the fog, Farrar knew his ship was doomed. Horrified, yet curiously calm, he had watched the brutal bow of the other vessel slicing towards them. A minute to live? Sixty seconds. But suddenly time stretched – the Rogue seemed to be inching forward as in a slow-motion film. Farrar could see everything very clearly. The looming ship was a tanker. He read the name – *Saracen.* It rang a faint bell in his head. He noticed that *Saracen*'s lifeboats were partly lowered. Expecting an accident? Captain Farrar wondered how he would save his own crew – if they weren't all blown to kingdom come. The radio operator continued sending an SOS. Farrar remembered his wife Mary . . .

At that moment, aboard *Saracen,* a uniformed figure grinned humourlessly. His eyes were glazed. No one heard him as he barely whispered: 'I'll get you, Farrar! I'll get you!'

Then the ships crashed. With a terrible shudder, *Olympus* buckled and split. Screams mingled with the din of mangling metal. Below, the engine room was flooding. Two men had been killed outright by the impact, three more were sucked through a jagged gash in the ship's side. On deck, the half-trained seamen panicked, rushing mindlessly, shouting. Some collapsed on their knees and moaned. A few prayed. Several sailors had tumbled overboard in the collision. One man fell, striking his head, and lay still. Farrar didn't know the full casualty list. His first officer and a dozen obedient crew members were trying to launch the lifeboats. But the winches had jammed. And *Olympus* was sinking, sinking . . .

Half an hour after, the rescue flotilla arrived. Now

only the bridge of *Olympus* showed above water. Gary saw men waving frantically. A billowing skirt of oil surrounded the stricken supertanker. Three helicopters were hauling up sailors from the fouled sea, and hospital ships began to collect survivors. *Saracen*'s officers and crew left their lifeboats and clambered aboard a tug.

Close to *Trident,* a figure was floundering in the brown waves. 'Quick!' barked the captain. 'Help him!' Two ratings scampered down a rope ladder to a dinghy and paddled towards the drowning man. They caught his arms, heaving him out of the water. Soon he lay gasping and coughing on a bunk in the captain's cabin. He looked Chinese. Dark liquid trickled from one corner of his mouth. 'Oil,' sighed the medical officer. 'Not much hope, I'm afraid. And there'll be plenty more like him.'

Perched near the bow, Gary scanned the hectic scene as rescue vessels went about their urgent mission. Amid all the activity, he had been momentarily forgotten. Gary stared hard at *Olympus*. The supertanker was going under! But someone was still on board – Captain Farrar. Would he be lost with his ship? A helicopter hovered over the tanker's bridge, dangling a line with a harness. Farrar hesitated, slipped the harness around his body, then rose in the air. Simultaneously, *Olympus* started to plunge – down to the bottom of the English Channel.

'Phew!' Gary gasped, watching the sea's surface swirl and bubble. 'What an escape!'

'Yep,' said the officer who had come up behind him. 'But, unfortunately, the trouble isn't over yet. In fact, it's only just beginning . . .'

CHAPTER FOUR

Suspicion

Several thousand feet up, a light aircraft circled above the rescuers. It had been patrolling like a vulture since the tankers collided. From his cockpit, the pilot had seen *Saracen* smash into *Olympus*, seen the Rogue's lifeboats launched, seen the flotilla arrive, seen Farrar's ship sink. Now the plane's pilot turned inquiringly to the well-dressed man beside him. 'Excellent – and most enjoyable,' purred a voice with a foreign accent. 'I can report that the first stage of our plan is a success.' The pilot pulled the control column, making the aircraft bank, and set course for France.

SUPERTANKER DISASTER – OIL MENACE GROWS. The big, bold headline on a London newspaper bill-board reminded John Jenkins that he had a tough task ahead. He pushed through the swing doors of Regal Maritime Insurance, nodded to the receptionist and strode towards the lift.

Two minutes later, he was sitting in his untidy fifth-floor office. His secretary was late again, he noted irritably. Frowning, he re-read the documents she had brought him yesterday afternoon. They were from the owners of *Saracen*, claiming £42 million – £10 million for the lost ship, £32 million for the oil cargo. Jenkins whistled softly at the size of the sum. Regal Insurance would go broke if it paid out many claims like that. But did Regal have to pay this time? Not if he could help it!

As an insurance claims investigator, it was his job

to be suspicious. And the *Saracen* case made him particularly so.

Jenkins lit a cigarette, his fourth in the last hour, and coughed till his eyes watered. He started writing notes on a desk pad. Then the door burst open.

'Morning, Mr Jenkins.' A short, plump, middle-aged woman with flushed cheeks gave him what she hoped was a winning smile. 'Good morning, Margaret,' he said. 'How about some coffee?'

'Coming right up,' his secretary chirped, and bustled off to fill the electric kettle.

Sipping black coffee from a chipped blue mug, Jenkins jotted down more notes about *Saracen* and thought of his coming interview with Richard Langley. The phone rang. Margaret answered it. Then, in a high, fussy voice, she said: 'Mr Langley will see you now.' Jenkins chuckled at her perfect imitation of Langley's la-de-da secretary, Gloria.

He stood up, towering over Margaret, and collected his papers. She inspected him critically. 'You can't go to see your boss looking like that,' she said, and began brushing cigarette ash from his rumpled brown suit. Standing on tiptoe, she straightened his tie. Jenkins had another coughing fit. 'Shouldn't smoke so much, Mr Jenkins,' she scolded. 'Don't I know it!' he agreed. 'Sooner or later, I'll kick the habit.'

Jenkins took the lift to the seventh floor. He walked briskly along the corridor and knocked on the door of Langley's office. 'Enter,' said Gloria's grating voice. Jenkins went in, passing the attractive redhead.

Langley was sitting in a padded leather chair behind an impressive mahogany desk. 'Ah, Jenkins, take a seat.' The tall, slightly stooping figure crossed what seemed like miles of red carpet and sat opposite his boss. Langley gazed coolly at the scruffy man before him. Aged forty, lean, with thinning sandy hair and penetrating blue eyes, Jenkins was a first-rate investigator. But almost too keen, Langley thought.

Jenkins returned the gaze. His boss was four years younger. A smart, ambitious man whose main interest in life appeared to be promotion. One day, Jenkins was sure, Langley would become Regal's managing director.

But they didn't like each other much.

'Well,' said Langley. 'I gather you want to talk over the *Saracen* claim. What's the problem?'

'It stinks. That's the problem.'

Langley wrinkled his pinched nose as though he could smell something unpleasant. 'Really,' he said with a disapproving air. 'It seems a fairly straightforward case to me.'

'Straightforward!' exclaimed Jenkins. 'Why, practically everything about it is suspicious.'

'What do you mean? Explain yourself, man.'

'Certainly.' The investigator shuffled his notes. 'Let's look at the circumstances of the collision. *Saracen* steams full speed ahead through dense fog in the wrong sea lane. Madness, flirting with suicide! Southead traffic control, which isn't expecting the ship's arrival, tries to raise the captain by radio. No answer. Other vessels in the vicinity, including *Olympus,* try to contact the Rogue. Nothing. Why? And what was *Saracen* doing in that part of the Channel anyway? The ship couldn't have docked at Southead without prior permission. But what really bugs me is the captain's behaviour. He must have realized the risk he was running – it's almost as though he *wanted* to crash.'

Langley shifted in his chair. 'If what you say is true, then I agree the captain acted . . . irresponsibly. Perhaps he didn't know *Saracen*'s position in the Channel, and maybe the ship's radio was out of action. But as for the collision being deliberate, well, that's ridiculous. What sane man would gamble with his own life and the lives of his crew? You've been reading too many crime stories, Jenkins.'

The investigator cleared his throat. His pale blue eyes glinted fiercely. 'Who said the captain of *Saracen* was sane?'

'Oh, you think he was out of his mind, a raving lunatic, eh?' sneered Langley.

'It's possible,' Jenkins replied. 'Besides, the whole business smells fishy. I heard that a French patrol vessel challenged *Saracen* earlier, but the tanker ignored her signals and fled into the fog. Then there's the helicopter pilot's report from the scene of the collision. He said he didn't spot a trace of oil where the Rogue sank, yet *Olympus* was bleeding the stuff all over the sea. Makes me wonder whether *Saracen* really was carrying an oil cargo – especially as the owners are asking Regal to fork out £32 million for it.'

Langley looked interested for a moment, but then said: 'Sorry. I'm still not convinced.'

Jenkins' temperature rose. 'I don't expect you to be,' he retorted, with more than a hint of sarcasm. 'Just let me prove it – or at least try. Or do you enjoy giving Regal's money away?' The investigator guessed that would stir things up.

'You've said enough, Jenkins!' His boss was white faced. 'Now listen to *me*. Of course I don't want Regal Insurance to pay out unnecessary claims. But we have a reputation to maintain. If our clients can't trust us to cover their losses when there's an accident, they'll insure their ships elsewhere.'

'Accident?' scoffed Jenkins. 'Some accident!'

Langley took no notice. 'We should be grateful *Olympus* wasn't insured by Regal, too.'

'This claim's crooked, I'm certain,' muttered the investigator.

Jenkins suddenly grinned. 'Look, Mr Langley. I know you are a busy man and good at your job. Why not just let me do mine?' With a sigh, he added: 'Maybe you're right. Maybe this case is on the level. But I can't help getting worked up at the possibility of someone cheating our company of £42 million. Besides, you'd look pretty silly if we paid out, and then it was discovered the claim was a fraud. Might give other clients wrong ideas.'

Langley nodded.

'As you know only too well,' Jenkins went on, 'there are four tanker accidents a week. It costs the insurers a fortune. But swindlers make it worse. Remember the big scandal earlier this year? A tanker said to have sunk with a cargo of oil, oil that had already been bought by a customer for £25 million. The ship owners claimed insurance. Then it turned out that the captain had stopped at a foreign port, re-sold the oil on the black market, and deliberately scuttled his empty ship. A tidy racket! And they'd have got away with it if an insurance investigator hadn't been suspicious.'

Jenkins paused. 'But, as you say, Mr Langley, the *Saracen* case is *probably* quite straightforward. Anyhow, it's your neck . . .'

Langley pursed his lips. 'Okay, Jenkins. Go to Southead. See what you can dig up. You've got a week.'

Jenkins feigned surprise. 'Thanks, Mr Langley.' He rose, gathering his papers. 'Goodbye,' he said, bowed slightly, and left the room. With a jaunty step, he headed for the lift.

'Well, did Mr Langley see sense?' Margaret asked.

'In the end.' Jenkins grinned foxily. 'Margaret, ring Regal's Southead branch and ask them to fix my accommodation for the next seven days. Then get my wife on the phone.'

The investigator went to a cupboard and removed a battered suitcase he kept packed for such trips. He checked the contents, adding some documents.

'Your wife, Mr Jenkins.' Margaret passed him the phone.

'Hello, Joan,' he said. 'I'm going to Southead for a while. The *Saracen* affair. Short notice, I'm afraid.'

The voice at the other end of the line protested: 'But we've arranged to go and hear Susan play her piano solo at the school concert tonight.'

'Damn,' said Jenkins. 'I'd forgotten. Give her my love and tell her I'm sorry. At least she understands her scatter-brained father.'

'All right, darling,' said his long-suffering wife.

'You can contact me through the Southead office,' added Jenkins. 'Margaret will give you the details. I'll call you every day.'

'Make sure you eat regular meals, John. And do try to cut down on the smoking – that cough of yours sounds awful. Take care, my dear, and good luck.'

'Thanks, Joan.'

Jenkins put down the receiver, sat gazing for a moment, then picked up his suitcase. 'Cheerio, Margaret. I should be at the Southead office by mid-afternoon.'

Jenkins took the lift to the basement car park. He climbed into his red Ford (badly in need of a clean), started the engine and drove up the ramp to the street. It was raining as he eased out into the London traffic. Saves washing the car, he thought.

Jenkins turned on the radio. Pop music, followed

by a news bulletin with up-to-date information on the Channel oil spill. An oil slick, twenty-five miles square and still spreading, was drifting towards the south coast of England. Jenkins clicked his tongue. There was more. Three seamen from *Olympus* lay critically ill in a Southead hospital. Poor devils! Jenkins switched off the radio.

Stopping at traffic lights, he stared grimly through the swishing windscreen wipers. *Saracen*'s captain – his name was Mercouri, wasn't it? – had a lot to answer for. The lights changed and Jenkins accelerated. His face set.

If there were big fish behind a massive insurance fiddle, Jenkins had no intention of letting them off the hook.

CHAPTER FIVE

Invasion

The heaving brown stain swelled hour by hour until it had invaded more than half the water between England and France. At 30,000 feet above the Channel, airline passengers craned their necks to get a better view of what now resembled a chocolate-coloured plain. From that height, the aircraft far below looked like models as they skimmed fifty feet above the sea, showering detergent on the oil. And amid the greasy waves, ships were also waging war against the creeping brown poison. Some sprayed chemicals while towing a series of paddles. This broke the oil into droplets so that bacteria in the water could 'eat' it easily. Elsewhere, other vessels encircled the oil with floating booms, then sucked it aboard through machines that separated oil from water. Airmen and sailors had combined to fight this deadly menace. But it was too big, too strong for them . . .

'Heaven help us if that lot lands!' Commander Izzard sat hunched over a two-way radio, following the progress of Operation Clean-Up. His gloom was shared by all the officers in Southead traffic control room.

But Lieutenant Mitchell said: 'It could be worse, sir. At least the wind's changed direction. With luck, the oil slick will drift along the Channel and miss the coasts.'

'Luck!' snorted Izzard. 'Not much of that about lately, Lieutenant.'

Mitchell didn't reply. In the background, he could

hear another officer alerting ships to steer clear of the cleaning area.

'Oil,' growled the Commander. 'I've seen a spill half the size of *Olympus*'s pollute 1,000 square miles of sea and coat 100 miles of golden holiday beaches in stinking slime a foot thick. And even if this slick doesn't come ashore, think of the damage it's already done. It could ruin our fishing industry.'

Mitchell wanted to say something, but Izzard had started a lecture. 'That tanker's still spewing out muck,' he added. 'The Navy will have to send down divers to try to plug those holes – double quick. Submerged wrecks can go on leaking oil for fifty years.'

'Fancy some coffee, sir?' Mitchell asked.

A twinkle dawned in Izzard's eyes. 'Anything to shut me up, eh, Lieutenant? Still, I could do with a cup. Thanks.'

Commander Izzard drained the last of his coffee and continued listening to the radio. He was feeling in a slightly better mood. Perhaps the oil *would* miss the land, though the odds against it were a thousand to one . . .

Eighty-three miles away, in London, an Admiral of the Fleet pointed to the Channel on a wall map. 'Gentlemen,' he said. 'We are facing a full-scale invasion. The enemy: 220,000 tons of crude oil. How are we going to beat it?'

There was a buzz of conversation around the long table in front of him. Experts from all over Britain had gathered at the Department of the Environment headquarters for this top-level council of war. Government Ministers and Army, Navy and Air Force chiefs sat side by side with biologists, naturalists, conservationists and anti-pollution specialists.

A Minister outlined the battle plan. Lorry-loads of detergent were being rushed to various coastal towns, he reported. From there, the cleaning chemical would be despatched to beaches fouled by oil. Fire-engines would pump out millions of gallons of the white liquid, then 'shampoo' the sand by hosing it with water, while farm machinery ploughed up the beaches to uncover oil that had seeped down deep. And helicopters would ferry drums of detergent to remote coves, where oil was likely to collect in pockets. These pockets must be cleared, the Minister explained, or else they would keep supplying the tides with more brown slime to dump on the newly-cleaned beaches.

'This is a major crisis,' he emphasized. 'England has had to deal with pollution before – but never on such a scale. Can we win? We've got to! If we don't, tourists will stop coming to our south coast. Millions of pounds lost, hotels closed, people out of work . . .'

Finally, forcing a smile, the Minister added: 'Of course, it's *just* possible the oil won't arrive.'

A harassed-looking man, an expert on the fishing industry, stood up. 'What I have to tell you, gentlemen, won't take long. Oil kills all life in the water – the fish and the food they eat. Even fish that escape may be affected, may not be able to breed, or may move to different seas. Our fishermen already find it hard enough to make a living because of growing competition from foreign trawlers and because the numbers of fish are dwindling. Now this oil spill! It could put some fishing fleets out of business.'

The expert sat down. No one spoke. Then the Admiral cleared his throat and said: 'Yes . . . well, not very encouraging. Let's hear from our bird man.'

Glaring at the Admiral, a naturalist rose to his

feet. He resented the fact that hardly anyone there seemed to care about the survival of sea birds – perhaps because birds weren't worth money.

'Sometime last year,' he began, 'a tanker illegally discharged a small amount of oil off Scandinavia. As a result, 100,000 sea birds died agonizing deaths – guillemots, gannets, puffins, razorbills, little auks, kittiwakes. The *Olympus* oil slick is thousands of times bigger than that other spill. Imagine the harm it could do.'

The naturalist paused to let his words sink in.

'Oil often sends birds blind,' he went on. 'It burns their skin, stomachs and livers. It also destroys the waterproofing of their feathers, which insulates them against cold and wet, so they can't float properly or catch fish. And if birds aren't poisoned by swallowing oil after preening, they'll probably die of pneumonia.'

He turned to the Minister, who was doodling on a pad, and said: 'The RSPB will try to save these pathetic creatures – even though many will die later, despite being cleaned. We've set up rescue stations along the coast. But we need Government support – money and volunteers. It's up to all of us to help. Otherwise some species of bird may become extinct.'

Politely, but without enthusiasm, the Minister agreed to ask the Government for aid. But he soon returned to the subject of the beaches. Shaking his head, he told the meeting: 'This pollution has come at the worst possible time. The peak holiday season is almost here. If the Devil himself wanted to sabotage our tourist trade, he couldn't have done a better job.'

The Admiral spoke last. 'Well, gentlemen, there's nothing more we can do – except keep our fingers crossed. But if the wind changes direction or a gale blows up, beaches are going to be ankle-deep in oil.'

That evening, after school, Gary finished fixing the sails to a model schooner he was building in his bedroom. He leant back, half closing his eyes, and imagined himself the master of a majestic sailing ship bucking and battering through raging seas. The crew and passengers were terrified. Only he, Captain Gary Izzard, could get them safely to harbour . . .

Gary chuckled, reached for his transistor radio and switched it on. The weather forecast. Most of Britain would remain warm with little or no wind, said the Meteorological Office. But the south must expect something different – gales. Gary opened the bedroom window. Down the garden, the branches of the apple trees were whipping in a fierce breeze.

He glanced at his watch. Should he do his homework now? Gary decided to go out for a while with his dog Snuff, a black springer spaniel. He changed into his track suit and sneakers, slammed the door behind him and galloped downstairs.

'Snuff . . . Snuffy!' he yelled. The dog appeared from nowhere, pink tongue lolling, stubby tail wagging. 'Good boy.' Gary fondled his pet's muzzle, and went into the kitchen.

'Where are you going?' asked his mother.

'To the beach, Mum.'

'All right, but don't be too long. Food's at seven.' She shook a warning finger, then smiled.

Gary and Snuff made for the front door, dodging the younger brother who would want to come with them. They left the house and started to run towards the beach, only a mile away.

As Gary ran, the wind pushed harder and harder against his chest. Once, Snuff was almost bowled over by a sudden gust. On the beach, they slowed to a jog-trot. Stopping, Gary picked up a piece of driftwood. 'Snuff! Fetch it, boy!' Eagerly, the dog tore after the flying stick.

But Snuff, usually an excellent retriever, didn't return with the driftwood. Instead, after several minutes, he padded back with a black shape dangling from his soft mouth. Gary squinted, puzzled. The dog dropped the strange burden at his master's feet. It was a sea bird, a cormorant, and it was dead. Gary stooped to examine the sad bundle of feathers. The body was sticky, smeared with grease. Then Gary noticed the dark slime clinging to his sneakers.

Thoughtfully, he walked on, Snuff beside him. They came to a rock pool. Floating on the surface, surrounded by brown streaks, were two fish.

There was no doubt about it – the oil had landed!

Back at home, Gary wolfed his meal. Mrs Izzard could hardly get a word out of him, and he completely ignored the chatter of his sister and kid brother.

Later, in the living room, he switched on the television. The Nine O'Clock News showed film of the oil invasion at various coastal resorts. Then there were pictures of slime-coated sea birds. An RSPB official was saying that people who found sick birds should take them to the nearest police station, and they would be told where to get expert help. 'Use a towel or something similar to cover the bird,' advised the official. 'It may try to bite, but this is never serious. To prevent a bird eating the tar on its feathers, an old sock with a hole cut in the toe can be pulled over its head.'

Next, reporters interviewed fishermen and owners of seaside boarding houses. Would the oil hurt their businesses? Certainly, they all agreed glumly.

The news bulletin ended with an item about the crew of *Olympus* – two more sailors had died.

Gary's throat tightened. He remembered the day of the collision, remembered travelling out to the wrecks and the feeling he'd had that the Rogue's captain was some kind of fiend. 'That man's wicked,' he muttered, wishing he could bring all the dead seamen back to life. *Saracen*! The name alone gave him goose pimples. This week, school broke up for the summer holidays. Gary would go to the beach. Maybe he could do a bit to clear up the terrible mess that was coming.

He thought again of *Saracen* and the mysterious captain. Why . . . why had it happened?

Gary wasn't the only one with *Saracen* on his mind. Investigator John Jenkins had considered little else since leaving Regal Insurance in London two days ago. Now, as he sauntered up to the bar of his Southead hotel, he felt quite pleased with himself. Jenkins' inquiries into the *Saracen* claim were already showing that he was right to be suspicious.

The insurance investigator sat down in an armchair and sipped a whisky and soda. I've earned this drink, he thought.

Jenkins reviewed the past few hours. In the morning, he'd spoken to Duncan Farrar, master of *Olympus*. Very interesting it had proved, too. Farrar, soon to give evidence in Southead Court, had described the collision carefully. He mentioned that the name *Saracen* seemed vaguely familiar to him at the time. He also said the Rogue's lifeboats were partly lowered before the crash and that, afterwards, those same boats had been rowed away with no attempt to save the *Olympus* sailors threshing in the oily water.

Jenkins liked Farrar, and found their talk useful. But the investigator was even more satisfied by what he learnt that afternoon. It was pure chance – a lucky break.

He had come across one of *Saracen*'s crew in a dockside pub. The man – Larsen – was drunk, and his tongue had been loosened. Jenkins leant closer to catch the blurred speech. '*Saracen* . . . a rust bucket,' Larsen blurted. 'Not fit to go to sea.'

Jenkins moved nearer still.

'And Mercouri,' the crewman spat, '*Captain* Mercouri – I'll swear he hit that other ship on purpose.' Just then, an officer from *Saracen* barged forward. He was big, built like a gorilla. Larsen paled. An iron grip held his arm, and he was led off . . .

Jenkins relaxed in his hotel armchair and finished the whisky. Yes, the *Saracen* investigation was going very nicely. Piece by piece, the puzzle was fitting together. An ugly picture – but it might mean that Regal Insurance didn't have to pay out £42 million.

Whistling, Jenkins took the stairs two at a time to his room. He unlocked the door and entered. The whistle faded from his lips. 'What the blazes . . . ?'

Chaos! His open suitcase lay upside-down on the floor. Tangled clothes were strewn everywhere. Wardrobe drawers had been rifled, then thrown aside. Even the bed was stripped.

Burglars? Unlikely, thought Jenkins. This search was thorough. He stepped over the debris, and picked up his document case. It, too, had been emptied. But the *Saracen* papers, with his notes, still lay nearby.

Slowly, methodically, he tidied up, checking his belongings. Nothing missing. Then why?

Bewildered, Jenkins sat on the bed and glanced at the window-side table. Call the police? Not much point, he decided. His gaze returned to the table, to a small space by the ashtray. An icy chill shot up his spine.

Something *was* missing – and its absence spelt real and sinister danger. Jenkins racked his brain, trying to remember. Yes, he definitely had put the photograph there. He always carried it with him when away from home. But now, the small colour portrait of his wife Joan and twelve-year-old daughter Susan had gone . . .

CHAPTER SIX

Battle of the Beaches

Jenkins' heart hammered. If any harm came to his family . . . He reached for the phone and dialled home. Long, long moments. But no answer. Why? He cut the connection and rang again. Come on, Joan! Still no reply. He checked his watch – 10.24. Maybe they were out or even asleep. Jenkins hung up. Should he drive straight back to London? He hesitated. No point in scaring Joan. Perhaps he *was* panicking. He'd call her first thing in the morning.

Feeling slightly dazed, he finished tidying his hotel room. In bed, disturbing thoughts chased each other through his mind. At last he drifted into sleep. But a nightmare ruined his rest . . . Joan and Susan being stalked by shadowy shapes.

A bell shrilled in his ear. Jenkins grunted, groping for the phone. 'Yeah,' he mumbled. The hotel receptionist sounded cheerful: 'Your morning call, sir. It's 7.30.' Suddenly, Jenkins was wide awake. The missing photograph! Phone home. Immediately. He dialled the number. It rang fifteen, twenty, thirty times. He replaced the receiver. What to do?

Jenkins hurried to the bathroom, took a shower and shaved. As he dressed, his mind juggled with the possibilities. Then he made a decision. He'd go to Regal's local office, where he had to collect some money and papers, and try once more to contact his family. If he couldn't raise Joan this time, he would leave Southead and speed home. And to hell with the *Saracen* investigation!

Jenkins packed his belongings, picked up his document case and went down to breakfast. Three quarters of an hour later, he had concluded his business at Regal Insurance. Now for that all-important phone call. The number kept ringing. His spirits sank. Then . . .

'Hello.' A familiar voice.

'Joan! Is that you?'

'Who else?' said his wife, laughing.

Jenkins struggled to keep an even tone. 'Where were you? I've been trying to get in touch with you since last night.'

'Mother's ill. I was with her, and I'll be staying there for the next few days. Why, is anything the matter, John?'

'Er, no. Nothing. I just happen to like talking to my wife and daughter sometimes.'

Joan chipped in: 'Well, you're the one who said he'd phone every day. And *this* is the first I've heard from you.'

Jenkins cleared his throat. 'I've been pretty busy, love . . . Anyway, how's Susan?'

'Fine, when I last saw her. That was yesterday morning.'

Jenkins' stomach clenched. 'Not since then? What about school?'

Joan sighed. 'Honestly, John, you never remember anything that isn't to do with work. The school term's over. Susan has gone to stay with Aunt Maude at the coast. You know our daughter – mad keen on birds – she wanted to help save them from the oil. She's quite near you, only six miles from Southead. Perhaps you two can get together.'

Silence. Jenkins' mind raced. So Susan was nearby. She might be safer here than at home – and he could keep an eye on her. Joan, too, would be better off at her mother's . . .

'John? Are you there?'

'Sorry, dear. Just thinking.'

'Well, what news – still smoking like a chimney? And any progress on the *Saracen* case?'

Ducking the first question, Jenkins replied: 'The *Saracen* claim's a phoney. I've got evidence of that now. I'll crack this case . . .'

'I'm sure you will, darling. Regal should double your salary.'

Jenkins chuckled. 'I agree. By the way, leave a message at the Southead office if you change your plans. I like to know where you are. Oh, and I'll ring Susan. You take good care of yourself, dear.'

'Of course, John,' said Joan, sounding a little surprised. 'You, too. Bye.'

The investigator sat back, chewing a pencil. Then he dialled his secretary, Margaret, in London.

'Punctual, for once,' he joked when she answered. 'Margaret, I've mislaid that colour portrait of my wife and daughter, the one I always take with me. Would you look on my desk and in the drawers?'

He waited.

'Sorry, Mr Jenkins. It's not there.'

'Okay. Thanks. Has my esteemed boss been asking after me?'

'No. But I gather from Gloria that Mr Langley thinks you're on a wild goose chase.'

'He would!' muttered Jenkins. 'But he's wrong. Anyhow, be sure to let me know if the photograph turns up. See you when I see you.'

A girl came in from the outer office with a cup of black coffee. Jenkins sipped it gratefully. Where *was* the picture? Maybe he'd left it at home, or dropped it somewhere.

No need to flap. At least Joan and Susan were safely out of the way. I must ring Susan. Jenkins resolved to spend more time with his family in future.

But for now, he had only one ambition – to bust the *Saracen* racket.

'The Battle of the Beaches has begun. Here, and along hundreds of miles of coastline, men and machines are attacking a deadly foe. Oil. A sticky, stinking slime that sweeps ashore with every tide. Driven by ferocious winds, this brown flood leaps the floating booms – intended to act as barriers – and pours on across sand and rocks. Even the once-white cliffs are stained and spattered . . .'

The television reporter continued talking as the camera swung away from his face to record the scene around him. To his right, 200 yards away, a helicopter swooped in a rush of sound, hovered, then rose with six drums of detergent dangling in a net. Ferrying its load to a distant cove, the helicopter looked rather like an eagle clutching its prey.

On the beach below, an army of figures swarmed amid miles of hosepipes gushing thousands of gallons of chemicals and water. Criss-crossing jets formed pools in the rocks, milky liquid mingling with brown, like chocolate blancmange and cream. But the smell was far from appetizing. Nearby, mechanical shovels dug up the beach. Later, when the sea was less polluted, bulldozers would shove the sand into the waves for further washing.

Meanwhile, off-shore, spraying ships kept up their assault on the advancing slick. Overhead, aircraft zoomed – some raining detergent, others co-ordinating the oil fighters at sea and on land or tracking the latest movement of the giant spill. Not surprisingly, no one took any notice of the light aircraft circling high above – the same plane whose occupants had watched with satisfaction as *Saracen* rammed *Olympus*.

By the water's edge, a team of firemen and soldiers concentrated their hoses on a stretch of rocks where a thick covering of oil clung like paint.

Not far away, Gary was trying to make himself useful. But the boy felt bitterly disappointed. Since breaking up from school, he had looked forward eagerly to joining the men in defeating the oil. At first, he was not even allowed on the beach – only Commander Izzard's influence had persuaded the authorities to relent. And now Gary was here, what could he do? Run messages, carry mugs of tea . . . 'Real hero's work!' he grumbled.

Shrugging his shoulders, Gary ambled towards the shore. He noticed a fair-haired girl, about his own age. Like him, she wore boots, jeans and a sweater. How does she come to be here? he wondered, and moved closer. The girl was crouching beside a uniformed RSPB officer. She was rather pretty, but her blue eyes were sad as she looked down. Gary followed her gaze . . . to a foot-long lump of tar. At one end, he could just see the gleam of red, yellow and blue stripes. A puffin. With their big multicoloured bills, white chests and cheeks, black backs, orange feet, short necks and dumpy bodies, puffins always made Gary want to giggle. But there was nothing funny about this oil-smothered corpse. To his surprise, he felt anger rising.

'Damned shame!' said the RSPB man. 'Ruddy tankers! Sea birds are the first to suffer.' He turned to Gary, then back to the girl. 'It's even worse in storms like the ones we've been having. You see, in rough weather birds seek the calmest water to rest on – and that's a patch of oil.'

The officer pressed a button on his walkie-talkie

and asked the rescue station for instructions. Several sick gannets had been sighted near the shore – would he help two other officers catch them? He pictured the handsome birds, usually snowy white, feverishly preening their grease-caked plumage. Rather curtly, he told the girl to meet him at the station in a couple of hours. Then, nodding to Gary, the RSPB man strode up the beach.

They stood in silence, the blonde girl and the dark-haired boy. Gary spoke first. 'That your father?' He indicated the officer's retreating back.

The girl smiled. 'No. The RSPB wouldn't let me wander round alone. I'm lucky to be here at all.'

Gary glanced at her lapel badge with its initials – BW – short for Beach Worker. He had one, too.

'What's your name?' he asked.

'Susan . . . Susan Jenkins.'

'I'm Gary.' He was going to shake hands, but felt silly. There was an awkward pause. Then they both started to talk at once, and laughed.

'How old are you?' asked Gary.

'Twelve.'

'I'm thirteen.'

'Well, I'm nearly thirteen,' Susan said quickly. 'How did you get permission to come on the beach?'

'My dad arranged it – Commander Izzard, in charge of Southead traffic control room. I was with him when the tankers collided, saw the whole thing on radar. Then I went out in a survey ship and watched the rescue. The crash was all *Saracen*'s fault. And as for the captain . . .'

Susan piped up. 'You should hear what *my* dad says about the captain! He's an insurance investigator, and he thinks the "accident" was fixed. But unless he can prove it, his company will have to pay out millions of pounds for *Saracen*.'

The boy said nothing, mind churning. Gary had been suspicious of the Rogue's captain. Susan's words brought back the memory. His brown eyes gleamed. He couldn't read the thoughts behind her blue eyes, but he guessed Susan felt it, too – they were linked by a mystery.

'Where do you live?' he asked.

'London. But I'm staying with my aunt in Belton for the holidays.'

'That's near me. You must come to my house. Meet Mum and Dad and Snuff, my dog. Afraid you'll have to put up with my brother and sister, though.'

Susan smiled, a little shyly. 'Thank you. I'd like to. I haven't got any brothers and sisters. Hey, maybe we could visit my father in Southead one day.'

'Great.' Gary gave a huge grin.

After that, the two new friends talked non-stop for an hour. Both agreed that they couldn't do much to fight the oil emergency, though Susan insisted she would keep trying to save the birds. Their conversation returned to the collision. Was there any way they could unravel the mystery? 'Seems impossible,' mused Gary. 'Even so . . .'

High above, the light aircraft kept prowling the sky. The pilot smirked as he and his wealthy passenger surveyed the brown stain spreading over the sea and slithering ashore on slimy tentacles. It was just too powerful for the oil fighters. 'A pretty sight,' gloated the cigar-smoking foreigner beside the pilot. 'As pretty as a billion pounds in gold.' The plane turned towards France, whose beaches had so far been spared the evil-smelling invasion.

Gary and Susan strolled by the water. Suddenly, Susan shivered. 'Cold?' asked Gary. 'No,' she said. 'Just a funny feeling – as if I'm being spied on.' Gary glanced around. Behind them, in the distance, the sun glinted for a second on something shiny. Glass? Binocular lenses, he decided. Probably some innocent birdwatcher who happened to be looking in their direction.

CHAPTER SEVEN

The Trial

Southead Court was packed. People wanted to see the man whose carelessness had caused a catastrophe. Who was this Captain Mercouri? A maniac? What would he have to say for himself? Would he be punished – if so, how severely?

Insurance investigator John Jenkins was as curious as everyone else sitting in the public gallery. He browsed through his notes on the *Saracen* claim and waited for the trial to begin. Mercouri was responsible for the collision – a tribunal had already established that. Now the Greek captain must explain his actions to a judge and jury.

Jenkins shifted his feet impatiently and surveyed the court. He recognized the dignified, grey-bearded face of *Olympus*'s master, Duncan Farrar. Poor chap looks worn out. Next to him sat a stocky figure in a commander's uniform – David Izzard, guessed Jenkins, father of Susan's new friend, Gary. Dear Susan; he'd missed her. Still, they would be seeing each other tomorrow afternoon, and he'd also meet Gary . . .

The trial was late starting. Jenkins fiddled with his watch strap. At last! The judge entered, and all in court stood up. An expectant hush. When everyone was seated, the judge directed his stern gaze to a square enclosure known as the dock. There, very soon, Mercouri would appear. Heads turned, voices murmured – a swarthy man, escorted by a court official, approached the dock.

Jenkins leant forward, staring, concentrating. So

this was the villain! Rapidly, the investigator took in every detail. Height: six feet. Build: broad. Age: around thirty-eight. Hair: dark, straight, greasy. Face: brown, pock-marked, scar on left cheek. Features: heavy eyebrows, hooked nose, thick, wet lips. But it was the eyes that riveted Jenkins' attention. They had seemed to look at him for a second. He would never forget them – black and burning with an unnatural brightness.

The clerk of the court rose, speaking. Mercouri was charged with gross misconduct and incompetence.

'How do you plead?' said the clerk. 'Guilty or not guilty?'

Mercouri glanced quickly at the defence counsel, the barrister who would defend him, and replied: 'Not guilty.' His voice was gruff and the accent difficult to understand.

Jenkins watched the Greek standing defiantly in the dock, his captain's hat tucked under his arm. 'Not guilty?' muttered the investigator. 'You're as guilty as hell!'

Before long, the prosecuting counsel was closing in on his target. Mercouri, said the prosecutor, had 'broken every rule of the sea, shown contempt for shipping safety. And the result? Two vessels sunk, massive oil pollution, thirteen lives lost . . .'

At the mention of his crew, Duncan Farrar went white. *Olympus*'s captain had spent most of last night by the bedside of a dying sailor in Southead General Hospital. From the public gallery, Jenkins could feel Farrar's pain. Mercouri should be facing a far more serious charge – manslaughter! Jenkins shot a look at the Greek, and was startled. Mercouri's eyes, glittering with hate, were glued to Farrar.

The prosecuting counsel put his case fully and then wound up.

Next, Commander Izzard was called to the witness box. In a clear, strong voice, he confirmed that the Rogue had ignored repeated warnings from Southead traffic control. *Saracen* had ploughed on through the fog in the wrong lane.

Then it was the turn of *Olympus*'s master to testify. Rather wearily, Duncan Farrar rose and crossed the court. A murmur of sympathy followed him. But there was nothing sympathetic about Mercouri's expression – his eyes stabbed Farrar in the back.

Quietly, with a slight Scottish accent, the pale captain gave his evidence. '*Saracen* wasn't sounding its fog horn,' he said,' 'and its lifeboats were partly lowered, too. After the collision,' Farrar's voice wavered for a moment, 'those boats could have picked up some of my men. But they didn't.'

Not a movement in court. Surely the Greek couldn't wriggle out of that.

The defence counsel was on his feet. 'My client, Captain Spiro Mercouri, barely speaks or understands English. Fortunately, I speak fluent Greek. So, with the court's permission, I will act as interpreter. Captain Mercouri has given me a full account of events leading to this tragic accident which, I need hardly say, shocked him deeply. To lose his own ship, and be involved in the loss of another, came as a particularly hard blow to so capable and conscientious a master as Captain Mercouri . . .'

Rubbish! Jenkins could hardly keep from exclaiming.

The smooth barrister continued his tall story. Mercouri had been unwell before the collision, was unaware of *Saracen*'s speed, the radio and radar were faulty, the tanker was lost in the Channel and trying to make for the Dutch port of Rotterdam.

Jenkins didn't believe a word of it. Nor did Commander Izzard, if his face was anything to go by. But several members of the jury looked at the Greek more kindly than before.

Time for the cross-examination. The prosecuting counsel pointed an accusing finger. 'What about Captain Farrar's testimony regarding the fog horn and the lifeboats?'

The Greek's eyes almost popped out of his head as he glowered at Farrar. Mercouri started to say something, but the defence counsel stepped in hastily. 'I will translate your question and my client's reply.' The white-wigged head of the barrister bent close to Mercouri's ear.

After a minute or two, the lawyer straightened up. 'Captain Mercouri has explained everything. *Saracen*'s crew was practising lifeboat drill, which is why the boats were partly lowered. Then, out of nowhere, came the collision. Captain Mercouri was badly shaken, not thinking clearly. But, as a good master, he knew his first duty was to save his crew. Somehow, in the confusion, he forgot the sailors from the other ship. *Saracen* did sound its fog horn, but the seamen on *Olympus* probably couldn't hear it because of their own fog horn.'

A long silence. Was *anyone* in court fooled? The judge took off his spectacles and wiped them with a handkerchief. Proceedings would adjourn for lunch, he declared, and the trial would resume at two o'clock sharp.

Gossiping excitedly, people filed out of the public gallery. But Jenkins remained seated, deep in thought. Without doubt, Mercouri would be found guilty. And the penalty? A heavy fine; maybe he'd lose his master's licence. Whatever happened, *Saracen*'s owners – Intercon, Inc. – would pay the bill and take care of the Greek captain. Regal Insurance still had to cough up £42 million! Unless Jenkins could prove the collision was deliberate. *Prove, Deliberate* – those were the key words. He recalled Larsen, the drunken crewman from *Saracen*. What had he said? That *Saracen* was a rust bucket, and that Mercouri meant to ram *Olympus*. Then the beefy bully had led Larsen off . . .

Yes, the crash was planned all right. But why? For the insurance money? Not worth the risk, Jenkins now decided. There had to be more to it, much more. Wherever he looked, the investigator kept seeing loose ends. One by one, he would have to tie them into a rope to lasso the men behind this fraud. If he failed, they'd get away with it.

Outside the court, Jenkins spotted Captain Farrar.

'Hello, Duncan.'

The Scot smiled wanly and shook hands.

'Must be a strain on you, the trial,' said Jenkins.

Farrar sighed. 'Can't say I'll be sorry when it's over, John.'

'That nutcase Mercouri's bound to be convicted,' added the investigator. 'But, unfortunately, Intercon will look after him.'

'Intercon?'

'The company which owns the ship.'

Farrar raised an eyebrow. 'That's a coincidence. I used to work for them. Intercon, eh? A shady outfit if ever I saw one. I couldn't wait to get out. Of course! I remember now why the name *Saracen* rang a bell – the tanker was being built when I left the company.'

Jenkins' mind whirred.

'Ever seen Mercouri before?' queried the investigator.

'Nope. I wouldn't forget that ugly mug. Why do you ask?'

'The way he was watching you in court. Talk about if looks could kill . . .'

Farrar frowned pensively, then shrugged. 'Beats me. Well, I must be going, John. See you later? I'll phone if anything occurs to me.'

'Thanks, Duncan.'

So Farrar had worked for Intercon. The Greek, too. A coincidence? In Jenkins' line of business there was no such thing.

Out at sea, oil still slurped like lumpy liquid chocolate. But, for the first time in days, it was not stirred by a strong wind. At last the gales had gone.

Over the wreck of *Olympus*, a 14,000-ton salvage vessel swayed lazily. On board, however, there was bustling activity. The ship's thirty-seven men – twenty crew, seventeen divers and underwater specialists – were preparing to tackle their toughest assignment. To help them, they had the most advanced equipment in the world. But would this be enough to stop the clouds of oil eddying up from the split supertanker 170 feet below? So far, storms had thwarted all diving attempts. Now, at least, they stood a chance.

In a cabin packed with electronic gadgetry, two salvage experts stared intently at the pictures on a television screen. Just a jumble of shapes and shadows. But then the experts spotted something – the dim outline of *Olympus*'s anchor. The pictures were being transmitted from a diving bell, slowly descending to the sunken wreck.

On top of the bell, a searchlight probed the murky Channel water, made even gloomier by billowing oil. Inside the bell, surrounded by technological aids, three frogmen prepared to venture out and explore *Olympus* at close quarters.

Soon they were gliding along the supertanker's quarter-mile-long hull, still miraculously in one piece. The trio of rubber-suited swimmers began to inspect the damage. Torches were little use against the swirling dark. But, within half an hour, the divers could confirm the bad news they had been told to expect – every one of *Olympus*'s thirteen tanks was ruptured, emptying its cargo into the sea. Somehow or other, the holes had to be plugged. About as easy as wrestling an octopus with your hands tied!

Meanwhile, several hundred yards away, two more salvage frogmen checked the wreck of *Saracen* which lay in slightly clearer water. The Rogue didn't seem to be leaking oil, only a little from the engine. Yet the ship's sides were gashed. Relieved but puzzled, the divers continued their survey. What they found completely baffled them.

This was no ordinary tanker. The bow was reinforced like an icebreaker's. Otherwise, *Saracen* was a rusting old tub.

Before leaving the Rogue's ungainly hulk, the two frogmen swam back to double-check the unusual bow. One of them, shining his torch, picked out the ship's name. Even that looked odd – as if painted over another name . . .

In the meantime, beside *Olympus*, the leader of the three-man diving party signalled his colleagues to return to the bell. Linked by a string of bubbles from their oxygen tanks, the black figures glided behind each other towards the yellow searchlight. Suddenly, though, the last man in line hesitated. What had he glimpsed out of the corner of his eye? Something bright, round, silvery. A trick of the light? Turning, he wriggled closer to investigate.

Clinging to the hull of *Olympus* was an object like an inverted metal soup plate. The frogman played his torch on it. A mine? Couldn't be. Then he knew – he had seen such a thing once before. It was a bugging device. With a powerful receiver, anyone could have tracked the supertanker at sea.

Eventually, using his knife, the diver managed to prise the device free. This chance discovery might prove vital! Kicking his flippers, the frogman headed after his two mates.

But he didn't reach the bell. Out of the gloom, without warning, a torpedo shape rushed at him. There was no time to dodge – no time for anything. As the midget submarine struck him, it knocked the air pipe from his mouth. Strangely, he felt no pain. Reeling, he struggled to stay conscious. A losing battle. The diver dropped what he was carrying.

Just for a second, as his eyes closed and darkness embraced him, he thought he saw a mechanical hand groping for the bright bugging device . . .

CHAPTER EIGHT

The Missing Portrait

'Ouch!' Susan sucked her finger and gazed reproachfully at the struggling bird. 'Now I know why you're called a razorbill.'

'Told you to be careful,' muttered the RSPB officer, saving his sympathy for the big black-and-white sea bird he was bathing. 'Anyway, it didn't hurt that much, did it?'

'Not really,' agreed Susan. 'Made me jump, that's all.'

She glanced around the brightly-lit rescue station. About thirty men and women were busy cleaning oil-glued feathers.

'Anything else I can do to help?' Susan asked.

'Not just now, thanks,' said the RSPB man. 'Try the others.'

Susan smiled, then wound her way between the wooden tables on which a variety of sea birds squawked, flapped or lay still. Some were being soaked in bowls of groundnut oil to loosen the tar. Others had already undergone this treatment, and were up to their necks in baths of hot water and detergent.

What's Gary doing? she wondered. Wish he'd hurry up and get here . . .

But it would be some time before Gary appeared. He was still on Belton beach, two miles away, near the home of Susan's Aunt Maude. And, at that moment, he was watching open-mouthed as a helicopter manoeuvred dangerously close to a cliff. The sun had set an hour ago, but batteries of brilliant floodlights made the night like day. The fat fuselage, long tail and whirling blades of the helicopter cast weird shadows on the sheer, white cliff wall. With incredible nerve and skill, the pilot inched the machine lower. Despite the risk, he must deliver his cargo of chemicals to a deep and narrow inlet where oil was massing for another assault on the sandy shores.

Belton beach was as crowded as it would have been on a normal sunny summer afternoon. But tonight, the teams of men working non-stop certainly didn't feel in holiday mood. An exceptionally high tide had thwarted them. Backed by howling winds, the oily waves had charged up the beach, laying a thick brown carpet of slime. So the sand and rocks were dirtier than ever.

Turning from the helicopter, Gary gazed along the floodlit shore. Nearby, six men in oilskins and goggles, their faces smeared with protective grease, wielded long hoses. One of them was shouting. Gary recognized the broad accent – a volunteer from the American Air Force base at Southead. All sorts of people had joined in the Battle of the Beaches. But was it a hopeless fight? Half-heartedly, Gary followed the progress of a distant tractor as it hauled a plough over the spoilt sand.

Usually cheerful, he couldn't find anything to raise his sinking spirits. He imagined the hot summer months. Who would want to come here on holiday – to sit or play on filthy beaches, paddle or swim in scummy water? What would it be like without British or foreign tourists? No one to ride the donkeys, visit the pier, take a boat trip round the harbour, buy toffee apples . . .

Sighing, Gary turned again to the helicopter, much lower now. It really was *very* near the cliff.

Suddenly, a great gust of wind tore in from the sea. Gary reeled. The wind hit the helicopter like a giant punch. Horrified, he saw the machine shudder and swerve closer to the white wall. Even from this distance, he could hear the blades screaming.

Then there was a sickening sound of metal on stone. Nose dipped, the helicopter hung motionless for a second . . . and fell like a dead bird. A ball of flame burst outwards and upwards, followed by a series of explosions. The pilot and crew had no chance.

Gary felt faint . . .

News of the crash took a minute to travel five miles to Emergency Headquarters at Southead Town Hall. When the phone rang in a dingy room, lined with maps, diagrams and aerial photographs of the spreading oil, a Civil Defence chief was briefing senior officers on Operation Clean-Up. Secretly, he thought the brown enemy was invincible. But, somehow, he had to inspire his exhausted men to redouble their efforts.

The CD chief answered the phone himself. His face, already haggard, looked ten years older as he replaced the receiver. Should he tell the others? No. They'd find out tomorrow. And they'd had enough bad news for one day.

Elsewhere in the town hall, another meeting was going on. An angry meeting. Several hundred people, including television cameramen and journalists, crammed the oak-panelled Council Chamber. They had been listening impatiently to a speech by an important politician, the Minister of the Environment, just back from his high-speed tour of the oil-swamped coastline. The Minister, a distinguished-looking figure in a pin-stripe suit, sat down and searched the audience for a friendly face. There wasn't one. His empty words had annoyed the men and women in front of him.

Then the questions started. 'Why isn't the Government doing more to combat the disaster? How will hotel owners, shopkeepers and everyone else who depends on holiday trade, earn a living? What about the fishermen whose boats are lying idle because it's not worth putting to sea?'

Flashbulbs popped as press photographers took pictures of the uncomfortable Minister. His answers satisfied no one. Finally, a woman in the second row loudly voiced the demand of most people present. 'We want action. Now! We want this mess cleared up quickly. And we want money from the Government – otherwise we'll all be broke by the end of the year.'

The perspiring politician promised to do everything in his power, and retreated from the meeting. He would have plenty to report to the Prime Minister in Downing Street next day . . .

At the rescue station, Susan stroked a big white gannet one last time before leaving. Outside, she breathed in the cool night air. The sky was strewn with sparkling silver stars, and the full moon seemed so close that Susan felt she could touch it if she stood on tiptoe. Her smile faded. Where *is* Gary?

Just then, a hand landed on her shoulder. Susan squealed, spun round. 'Idiot! You nearly scared me to death . . . and why are you late?'

Gary looked sheepish. 'Sorry.' He also appeared pale, thought Susan, but perhaps that was the moonlight.

'You okay?' she asked, more gently.

Gary told her about the helicopter crash as they shuffled across the beach towards the road. Susan listened in silence. Gary stopped talking, and they trudged along the lamplit road. His mind went back to the day he had spotted the Rogue on radar. He remembered the lost crew of *Olympus* and the men in the burnt-out helicopter. Susan was thinking of the birds.

'Mercouri!' Gary and Susan exclaimed together. They stared at each other in surprise.

'He's to blame,' muttered Susan. 'Him and that rotten *Saracen*.'

'Yeah,' agreed Gary. 'But I bet you he gets off lightly at the trial.'

'Maybe,' said Susan. 'My dad'll keep after him, though.'

'Wish we could help, Susan.'

'How *can* we?' The girl sounded tired and a little irritable.

'I dunno. At least you can keep track of what's happening through your father. And I'll pick *my* dad's brains. By the way, you'll like him a lot.'

'I'm sure I will.' Her smile wiped away the grumpiness.

They had almost reached the Izzards' house, where Susan was to stay overnight.

'Hang on a minute.' Susan leant against a fence. 'Got a stone in my shoe.'

Gary waited, gazing back down the road. With a slight shock, he noticed someone standing under a lamp post. The man, wearing a black leather jacket, was lighting a cigarette. I've seen him before, thought Gary. But where? He's not a local.

Gary and Susan continued walking. Once, the boy peeked over his shoulder. The man sauntered along a few yards behind. 'Let's get a move on,' urged Gary. Susan obeyed without comment. When Gary looked round again, the man had increased his pace, too.

Home, at last. Gary directed Susan through the front gate, pausing as he shut it.

The man passed by, whistling nonchalantly.

Gary grinned. Surely his vivid imagination was playing tricks. Who'd want to follow *them*?

Across the sea, in the great German port of Hamburg, tugs cleared their throats noisily as if to rouse the lines of sleeping ships. But the moored vessels of all nations drowsed on under a starry sky.

Behind the docks, the city was wide awake. In the Reeperbahn, a street dazzlingly decorated with neon signs, crowds flocked to restaurants and night clubs. The well-dressed man who slipped quickly into a club looked like any one of a hundred other people out to enjoy themselves. He descended the stairs, parted a bead curtain and entered a smoky cellar. In the dim blue light he could see cloth-covered tables where figures sat drinking, laughing, chatting and watching the spotlit cabaret.

The man joined in the applause for a knife-thrower who had just finished his act. Then, instead of ordering a drink, he crossed the room and pushed the door through which the performer had left.

'Hans!' The German knife-thrower turned at the sound of his name. He put a finger to his lips and beckoned the speaker. Soon they were sitting in a dressing room behind the stage, each with a glass of schnapps.

'What brings *you* here, Achmed? It must be serious.'

'Hans, the company has an urgent job for you.'

The performer sipped his drink. 'Well . . . ?'

'Larsen, one of *Saracen*'s crew. He's been shooting his mouth off. It has to be shut – permanently. You're to go to England . . .'

'A pleasure, Achmed. But why me and not someone on the spot?'

'You're an outsider. Unknown. And you can vanish afterwards.'

'It's as good as done, my Arab friend.' The performer momentarily gripped the ivory handle of a throwing knife. 'Tell me, what of that nosy insurance investigator?'

'Ah, yes. Jenkins. He's getting close, dangerously close. But I think we can persuade him to be a good boy . . .'

The German cocked an inquiring eyebrow.

The Arab reached into his inside jacket pocket and pulled out a photograph – a colour portrait of Susan and her mother.

CHAPTER NINE

Get moving!

'This way, Mr Jenkins. You're expected.' The tall investigator followed the staff nurse along a neon-lit hospital corridor which smelt strongly of disinfectant. He thought back to the phone-call that had brought him here, a tip off from a Navy contact.

'In there,' said the nurse, opening the door of a private room. 'You can't stay long, I'm afraid. Doctor's orders.'

Jenkins nodded his thanks and entered. Before him was a bed. One glance told him that the man between the sheets was ill, very ill. Beside the bed sat another figure. A diver, like the patient. The investigator introduced himself and took out a notebook.

Quietly, the second diver described how he'd saved his friend from drowning by the sunken wreck of *Olympus*. 'I'd finished checking *Saracen*,' he recalled. 'Then I swam over to see if I could help the main salvage team. Lucky I did! That's when I found Jim in trouble. He'd lost his air pipe. I towed him to the diving bell.' There was a pause. 'Just hope he pulls through . . .'

A shuddering moan rose from the bed. The patient, soaked in sweat, tossed and turned feverishly. Suddenly, he clutched his friend's arm. Jenkins moved closer as the sick man began to babble. 'The device . . . I *had* it!' Jenkins strained forward. 'What device? Tell me, Jim!' The injured diver trembled, twisting violently. 'N . . . no . . . Submarine . . . Must escape!' Releasing his grip, he fell back on the pillow, eyes blank.

At that moment, the nurse came in. 'Time to go, gentlemen.' Her brow furrowed. She approached the bed and felt the patient's wrist. Fever and shock had made his pulse pound. As Jenkins and the other visitor left, she prepared a sedative.

In the corridor, the two men conferred.

'What do you make of that?' asked Jenkins.

'It was after the dive. He'd just come to, then he blurted something about a bugging device on *Olympus*. Poor devil must've been delirious. He started yelling, said he was attacked by a midget submarine. I saw nothing. It's crazy.'

Jenkins stiffened. 'Is it?'

'You mean . . .' The diver shrugged. 'This whole salvage job is pretty weird, if you ask me.'

'Why?' Jenkins pricked his ears. 'What else?'

'Take *Saracen*. A rusty tub – yet it had a reinforced bow. And there was no oil cargo . . .'

The investigator's mind buzzed. His suspicions were proving right. 'Go on, man.' Jenkins listened eagerly. Then he said: 'Thanks. That's worth a lot. Maybe a fortune to Regal Insurance.'

'Don't mention it. Pity I can't help my pal, too.'

The nurse returned. 'He's resting now.' She smiled kindly. 'Your friend's had a bad time. But, with care, he'll mend.'

Minutes later, the investigator was seated behind the wheel of his Ford. He felt a twinge of excitement. So *Saracen* was an empty hulk. The bugging device, the submarine . . . extra evidence of a plot. At last, something solid to work on, something more than hunches and hearsay. This was the big break he'd been waiting for. A wolfish grin spread across his face.

Jenkins slammed the car into gear and pulled away, tyres squealing.

Like her father, Susan was in a good mood that morning. But unlike him, she was still dawdling over breakfast. Contentedly, she listened to the chatter around the Izzards' dining room table – so different from her own home, where she was the only child. She couldn't understand why Gary grumbled about his brother and sister. They seemed very nice. And Commander and Mrs Izzard were terrific.

Susan nibbled a piece of bacon.

'Eat up, dear.' Mrs Izzard smiled, indicating Susan's plate. 'Otherwise you'll be starving by lunch-time.' The girl tucked in.

There was a scrabbling at the door followed by several thuds. The handle jerked and the door swung open. A black dog padded into the room. 'Snuff – you know you're not allowed in here!' Mrs Izzard tried to sound cross, but it wasn't very convincing. 'Wretched animal's learnt to jump up and turn the handle,' she explained.

Gary winked at Susan. 'Can't he stay, Mum? He's no bother.'

'Oh, all right. But no scrounging food. Hear that, Snuff? You've already had *your* breakfast in the kitchen – enough to feed a lion.'

Commander Izzard asked for the marmalade, and Snuff was soon forgotten. The springer spaniel snuggled at Susan's feet. She stretched down to fondle his ears. He licked her hand and then sat up and begged. His imploring gaze pierced Susan's heart. Pretending to drop her napkin, she quickly slipped Snuff half a sausage. But the click of his teeth gave the game away. Gary's younger brother giggled as he caught sight of Snuff licking his chops guiltily. Susan blushed. Silence at the table. Then everyone laughed. 'That dog!' sighed Mrs Izzard. 'He'll burst one day.'

Snuff trotted over to his master, Gary, and breakfast resumed. Commander Izzard grinned at Susan as he buttered another piece of toast.

'Dad, what's the latest on the trial?' asked Gary.

The Commander's pleasant expression vanished. 'Not good, son. Mercouri's as crooked as a corkscrew; a nasty bit of work. But he won't get the punishment he deserves.'

How like his father Gary looked, thought Susan. This reminded her of her own father, and she wondered what he would have to say when they met that afternoon.

'Well, off to work.' Commander Izzard rose. 'A pleasure to make your acquaintance, young lady.' He reached across the table and squeezed Susan's hand. 'I hope we see more of you during the holidays. You're welcome here any time. Keep my daft son out of mischief, if you can.' He ruffled Gary's hair.

After the Commander had left for Southead traffic control, Susan helped clear away the breakfast things.

'Shall I wash up, Mrs Izzard? I often do at home.'

'No, that's all right, dear. Gary says you're quite a pianist. Perhaps you'd like to try our piano?' Mrs Izzard bustled off to the kitchen.

Susan smiled and sat at the keyboard of the upright piano. Snuff followed Gary to the window, while his brother and sister went upstairs. 'Play us something I can whistle,' said Gary, tickling his dog under the chin. Susan struck up a sea shanty, and Gary joined in with gusto. Then, in mid-note, he broke off. The girl turned towards him.

'Anything wrong, Gary?'

'See for yourself.'

She hastened to the window.

'There.' He pointed down to the road. 'Recognize him? The man in the black jacket.'

'Er . . . I'm not sure. Wasn't he walking behind us last night?'

'Trailing us, more like.' Gary shivered. Now he knew why the man under the lamp post had seemed familiar – he'd seen him twice before, by the rescue station. And the spying binoculars on the beach! Suddenly Gary was certain they belonged to the figure lurking below.

'What do you mean?' Susan's blue eyes were wide.

'He's after us.' Gary voiced his tumbling thoughts.

But the girl wasn't convinced. 'Surely not. Why?'

'Search me. But I've got a feeling it's connected with the *Saracen* mystery . . .'

Susan blinked nervously. 'Supposing you're right – what shall we do? Tell your parents?'

'No – at least, not yet. Don't want to worry them. They probably wouldn't believe it anyway. We'll tackle this on our own.'

Stealthily, Gary took a last look out the window. The man was still there. 'Right, let's get moving,' said Gary. He opened the door for Susan and called Snuff to heel.

In the kitchen, Mrs Izzard had just finished the washing-up. 'Hello, you two. Going to make the most of this lovely sunshine?'

'Um . . . yes.' Gary found it hard to meet his mother's gaze. 'Mum, could we take some sandwiches?'

'Of course, dear. Ham and tomato for you. And what would Susan like?'

'Cheese for me, please.'

A few minutes later, Gary and Susan stole out of the house by the back door. They took the dog with them. His keen hearing and marvellous sense of smell might prove useful. Faithful Snuff, so gentle – unless someone threatened Gary!

From the kitchen window, Mrs Izzard watched as the children crept through the gate at the bottom of the garden and into the long grass of the field beyond.

Meanwhile, four miles away, a dusty car screeched to a halt outside the Southead branch of Regal Insurance. Grabbing his document case, John Jenkins crossed the pavement in several long strides. Inside the building, he made straight for a quiet office. Wild goose chase, eh? I've got news for you, Langley.

The investigator dialled his boss in London. 'Mr Langley's secretary.' Gloria sounded as prissy as ever. 'Jenkins speaking. Put me on to Mr Langley.' Gloria hesitated. 'I'll see if he's free.' Jenkins pulled a face.

After a short delay, Langley came on the line. 'Glad you called, Jenkins. Your week's up. I want you back here.'

The investigator's jaw dropped. 'But . . . the *Saracen* claim! Haven't you read my reports? They've been telexed to you every day.'

'Don't amount to much, do they?'

'There's fresh evidence. It could clinch the case.'

'You've had your chance. Face it, you gambled and lost.'

Jenkins ground his teeth. 'Will you at least give me a hearing?'

'Very well. But my mind's made up.'

The investigator spelt out all he'd learnt at the hospital.

Langley snorted. 'Sounds pretty far-fetched to me. And as for *Saracen* being a rust bucket . . . that's absurd. The tanker was in perfect condition when we insured it three months ago.'

Jenkins fought the temptation to shout. 'I know that as well as you do, Mr Langley.'

'So what are you suggesting, man?'

'Try this for size. There are two *Saracens* – a modern oil-carrier and a rusting tub at the bottom of the Channel.'

No comment from Langley, then: 'Sink an empty old ship, pretend it's a loaded new one, and claim the insurance. Is that it? Makes no sense. Why risk an explosive collision near land? Why not just scuttle the vessel in deep water?'

Now it was Jenkins' turn to pause. 'I can't answer that – yet,' he admitted. 'But I'll find out. There's much more to this than an insurance fiddle.'

'I've listened long enough, Jenkins. Be in my office at ten o'clock tomorrow morning.'

The investigator's voice was tight. 'If I come back, I'll bring my resignation. Give me a few more days, and I'll save Regal £42 million. Your choice.'

'That's blackmail,' Langley spluttered. 'All right. One week. Not a day longer. And I want results – your job's at stake!'

There was a click, then the dialling tone. Jenkins hung up. A week! Could he keep his promise? Most of the puzzle was complete, but some pieces still didn't fit. What was Intercon's game? Did Mercouri have a grudge against *Olympus*'s Captain Farrar? If so, why? No shortage of questions. Just as well you don't need a lot of sleep, Jenkins.

It was then that he remembered he'd arranged to see Susan and her friend after lunch. Damn. Can't afford the time now. Guiltily, Jenkins thought of their other cancelled meetings. Still, he would make it up to his daughter later. And Susan was safe enough with her Aunt Maude and the Izzard family. Or was she? The missing photograph flashed in his mind's eye . . .

CHAPTER TEN

Murder

Snuff barked. Gary's hand shot out, closing round the dog's muzzle. 'Ssh! We're escaping. It's a secret.' Snuff's intelligent eyes searched his master's face. Though the words weren't understood, the message was. The dog didn't bark again. Susan crawled beside them as they moved on through the concealing grass.

The sun was hot, and she already felt sticky. A strand of blonde hair clung to her forehead. 'Brilliant idea of yours, Gary. Pity we can't do this all the time.'

'Keep your voice down!' he hissed. 'And there's no need to be sarcastic. We've got a spy on our tail.'

'So *you* say,' Susan sniffed scornfully. 'But what if you're wrong?'

'Want to go back and find out?'

No reply.

Snuff sprawled panting in the grass, looking from one to the other. At last the dog stretched, got to his feet and slowly headed off on his own. With a sudden smile, Susan pinched Gary. Soon the two friends had caught up with Snuff. Now they were only a hundred yards from a wood.

Minutes later, they stood under a cooling sunshade of branches. 'Phew,' puffed Susan. 'No wonder babies walk as soon as they can – crawling's hard work.' She flopped down on a tree stump and peered about her. If there *was* a spy, they'd certainly given him the slip. Susan giggled at the thought of the man still hanging around outside the Izzards' house.

'What's the time, Gary?'

He checked his watch. 'Elevenish.'

Susan opened her lunch bag. Gary squatted nearby and started munching a ham and tomato sandwich. Snuff prowled hopefully between them. But they were both surprisingly hungry, and the dog was out of luck.

'I could do with a drink,' said Gary.

'Me, too. A lovely big ginger beer with ice. My dad'll treat us when we get to Southead. How far is it?'

'About three miles.'

'Do I look a mess?' Susan brushed the dust off her jeans.

'No more than usual.'

Susan took a good-humoured swipe at him. Gary grinned. He was beginning to enjoy himself.

Suddenly, Snuff growled. His master froze. The dog crept forward, hackles bristling. A twig snapped behind them. Susan's heart beat faster. Gary sprang upright. Who . . . what . . . had made the noise? They listened – and heard something else. Snuff bared his teeth. It was closer than before. 'Get ready to run,' whispered Gary.

Seconds passed, seeming like minutes. Then a grey shape streaked into view. There was a flash of white as it vanished in the undergrowth. A rabbit. Snuff gave chase. Gary called him to heel, and the dog reluctantly returned.

A false alarm. But Susan was still shaking when they set off again. She'd be glad to see her father – he always knew what to do in any situation. Gary, too, had lost his cheerfulness. They must never forget that someone was after them, must stay on their guard.

Travelling cross-country, out of sight of the road, they reached Southead in just under two hours. Gary and Susan spent another half hour searching for her father's hotel – The Grand. Eventually, an obliging traffic warden directed them to a shabby building which didn't live up to its name. Outside, Gary and Snuff waited impatiently while Susan tidied her hair and picked grass seeds off her T-shirt. 'Come on,' grumbled Gary. 'You're not entering a beauty contest.'

The boy, the girl and the tousled black dog went in. At the hotel reception desk there was a further delay. The receptionist, a heavily made-up young woman with red-painted nails, ignored the group in front of her. So Gary banged the brass bell on the counter. Susan looked uncomfortable. The woman stared at Gary, then glared as she spotted Snuff. The springer spaniel wagged his tail.

'What do you want?' snapped the receptionist.

'Mr John Jenkins,' mumbled Susan, 'I'm to meet him here.'

'Ah, you'll be his daughter,' said the woman. 'He left something for you.' She handed over an envelope.

Susan tore it open and read: *So sorry I can't make it today. Too much work. We'll get together soon, I promise. Please apologize to your friend Gary. Have fun spending this £5 note. I'll phone you tonight. Love, Dad*

Susan showed the letter to Gary. She was grateful for the money, but she would far rather be with her father. And not just because she missed him. Susan now believed in the spy . . .

Two days later, the people of Southead and other south coast towns heard their first good news since the tanker collision. Divers from the salvage ship had done the 'impossible' – sealed the leaking wreck of *Olympus*. Oil no longer billowed upwards. A Navy submarine had guarded the rubber-suited swimmers. After the earlier incident with the frogman, no one was taking any chances.

Good news, too, from the oil fighters on land. The Battle of the Beaches was gradually being won, said the Commanding Officer. 'Yard by yard, we're re-capturing our shores.' But would the war be over in time for the peak holiday season?

In his hotel room, investigator John Jenkins grunted with satisfaction as he listened to the radio report. Full marks, Operation Clean-Up! He switched off the radio. Back to the *Saracen* claim. Regal Insurance needn't pay one penny – if he could prove the Rogue was an unseaworthy hulk. Easy. The master of the salvage vessel should be able to provide that evidence. Then Regal would tell Intercon, 'Hard luck!'

But Jenkins wasn't content with saving his company £42 million. The investigator wanted more – justice. He remembered the injured diver. The merciless men of Intercon were playing a dirty game. Jenkins intended to see they lost.

His thoughts turned for a moment to his family. Susan had sounded a little strange on the phone – but that was probably because she was disappointed at not seeing him the day before yesterday. Anyway, they really would meet today. And when he had called Joan at home, she'd been as happy as a lark. No, he didn't have to worry about his family.

Leaving the hotel, Jenkins drove straight to an appointment with Superintendent Compton. He was sure the police would share his enthusiasm for putting Intercon's crooks behind bars.

On Belton beach, Susan acted innocent as she sidled up to Gary with a handful of dripping seaweed. But he wasn't fooled, and ducked just in time.

'You and your spy!' she teased. 'Thank goodness we didn't tell our parents – we'd have looked proper idiots.'

Gary said nothing. They had seen no further sign of the man in the black leather jacket.

'I think I *will* tell my father at lunch.' Susan skipped mischievously. 'He could do with a laugh.'

'Please don't, Susan.'

The girl stopped teasing. 'Course not. Why so glum?'

'Well, I still feel we were being watched.'

'Come on, Gary. Forget it. These are the holidays. Let's have some fun. I vote we go to Southead fair and spend what's left of that fiver my dad gave us.'

Gary's eyes lit up. 'Even *you* have good ideas sometimes,' he said.

At the police station, a young woman constable ushered Jenkins into Superintendent Compton's office. 'How do you do.' Compton's handshake was a bone-cruncher. 'Sit down.'

The investigator regarded the bald figure across the desk, as tall as Jenkins and with the same shrewd eyes. 'Cigarette?' Jenkins accepted, noting that this office was almost as untidy as his own in London. The superintendent looked tired.

'Right, what can I do for you?' he said.

Jenkins briefly outlined what had happened since he first received the *Saracen* claim. 'It smelt bad from the start, and the stink has got worse and worse,' he concluded.

Superintendent Compton choked on the smoke from his cigarette. 'Quite a story,' he wheezed. 'If it's true, that Greek captain was damned lucky to get off with a £1,000 fine.'

Jenkins frowned irritably, recalling the unsatisfactory result of the trial. 'That's true, all right!' He felt like kicking something, or somebody – preferably Mercouri.

'I'm inclined to believe you, Mr Jenkins. But, unfortunately, there's not much the police can do. Intercon's a foreign outfit – we can't touch it without help from the authorities in other countries.'

The insurance investigator tried to hide his frustration.

'Besides,' Compton went on, 'we're already up to our ears in work. An enormous property swindle is being hatched. We *must* strangle it at birth. Otherwise Britain could lose many millions – maybe billions – of pounds. I won't bore you with the details. Let's just say certain greedy characters abroad are scheming to take over England's south coast holiday resorts and build hotels, gambling casinos, yacht marinas. What makes me even sicker is that these rich creeps have influential friends over here – people they've bribed.'

Property swindle? A faint light flickered in Jenkins' mind. Ships and oil were only part of Intercon's business. Didn't the company also own property around the world? He was still pondering this when the superintendent dropped a bigger bombshell.

'And on top of all that,' sighed Compton, 'we've got a murder to solve.'

Jenkins straightened his back.

'A particularly messy murder,' continued the superintendent. 'Come to think of it, you might be interested. The victim is – was – a sailor from *Saracen*. Name of Larsen.'

Larsen! The investigator swallowed hard. Breathlessly, he described the crewman he'd met in the dockside pub.

'Yes, that sounds like him,' said Compton. 'You'd barely recognize the poor devil now. Someone did a thorough job on his face with a knife.'

Jenkins pressed the superintendent for more information. Larsen had been discovered that morning when he fell out of a cupboard at the seamen's hostel where the crew was staying. No one there could offer any clues.

'Know him well?' asked Compton.

'No.' Jenkins' voice was low. 'Hardly at all. But he was the one who told me things about *Saracen* – things the captain wanted hushed up . . .'

Compton's eyes narrowed. 'So you think . . .'

'He may have died because he talked to me.'

'Hmm.' The superintendent rubbed his chin. 'It's possible. I'll be getting in touch with you later. Meanwhile, we've both got plenty to do. Sorry I can't help with the Intercon affair.'

Jenkins rose, his mind threshing. 'You *have* helped, Superintendent. Thanks. I've a feeling I can be useful to you, too.'

They shook hands.

In his car, Jenkins jotted down some notes. He felt sad and angry and determined at the same time. Larsen . . . murdered! By an Intercon thug? For blurting a few drunken words?

The investigator threw aside his notebook, started the engine and eased away from the kerb. He would *not* drop this case – whatever Langley said. Weaving through the traffic, Jenkins headed for Regal's Southead branch. There were facts he needed to check: for example, was Intercon involved in world-wide property deals?

Without knowing it, Jenkins passed the bus bringing Gary and Susan into town. The two friends jumped off at the depot. Soon they were jogging towards the sea front, Gary leading. They came to the promenade. At one end was the fair. They could see the big wheel, the helter-skelter, the ghost train . . .

'Race you!' Susan rushed ahead, her hair flying. Gary caught up just as they reached the fairground. Puffing, they stood outside the entrance gate. It was closed, padlocked.

'What a drag!' Gary stuffed his hands into his pockets and peered wistfully between the bars of the gate.

'Sorry, young 'uns.' A man in a peaked cap emerged from a hut. 'The fair won't be open for another fortnight. And maybe not then, if there aren't more customers. Blame the oil. It's kept holiday-makers away.'

Susan raised a half-hearted smile. 'Never mind, Gary. I'll treat you to a candy floss.' They wandered back along the promenade. 'Anyway,' said Susan, 'not long now before we get together with my dad.'

At the Regal office, investigator Jenkins dialled a London number. His old school chum Maurice Rosenburg was an expert on international business affairs. 'Maurice . . . John Jenkins here. I want to ask a favour.' Rosenburg listened, then left the phone. Jenkins drummed his fingers on the desk. 'Hello. Yes, Maurice . . . How many? . . . You sure? That's *very* interesting. Remind me to buy you a fat cigar.' They said goodbye.

Jenkins smiled grimly as he considered what he'd just heard. Intercon *did* have investments in property – even more than in ships and oil . . .

Then, as he was about to leave, the phone rang. He answered it.

'Mr John Jenkins?'

'Speaking.'

'You don't know me. But I was a friend of Kurt Larsen, his best friend. I have information for you.'

The investigator was wary. 'I see. And your name is?'

'Donovan. Listen, I can't talk long. I'm in a pub – The Lobster Pot – not far from you. Meet me here at one o'clock.'

Jenkins hesitated, suspecting a trap. 'Why should I trust you?'

'Because I'm risking my neck. They killed Kurt . . .'

'All right. What's this information?'

'Can't explain. No time. But if you want the truth about Intercon and that swine who calls himself Mercouri, be at The Lobster Pot.'

'How will I recognize you?'

Donovan described himself and his clothes, then hung up.

Jenkins paced the floor restlessly. Now the trial was over, *Saracen*'s crew could be shipped out any day. He *had* to take a chance . . .

Lost in thought, the investigator hurried to his car.

At her father's hotel, Susan pushed the revolving door and joined Gary in the foyer. 'The Grand . . . what a dump!' she giggled. Gary eyed the reception desk, remembering the snooty receptionist. But a different woman – older, kinder-looking – was on duty today.

The youngsters had almost reached the desk when John Jenkins strode in through the entrance.

'Susan!'

She turned, 'Dad!' and ran to hug him. Gary walked slowly behind her.

Holding his daughter's hand, Jenkins said: 'Well, introduce me to your friend.'

'Sorry. Gary, this is my father.'

Jenkins clapped Gary on the back. 'We meet at last. I've heard a lot of good things about you.'

For some reason, Susan went pink. She quickly asked: 'When are we going to eat, Dad? I'm starving. So's Gary.'

The tall investigator shifted his feet awkwardly. 'Er . . . bit of a problem, I'm afraid. Urgent appointment. I can't really take you along.'

'Oh, Dad!' A variety of expressions crossed Susan's face. 'Where is it, this appointment?'

'A pub – The Lobster Pot.'

Gary spoke up. 'I know the place. Serves smashing grub, indoors or out in the garden.'

'You see,' Susan tugged Jenkins' sleeve, 'we *can* come after all.'

'No, you don't understand,' her father protested.

Susan looked both stubborn and close to tears. 'I understand,' she mumbled. 'I wait ages to see you and then when I do, you go off to work again.'

Jenkins caught her accusing stare, softened by a silent plea. 'Okay,' he sighed. Against his better judgement, he agreed to take the children with him.

In the dusty Ford, Susan chattered happily beside her father as he drove. From the back seat, Gary gave directions to The Lobster Pot. Susan told Jenkins about the wasted trip to the fair. Her father tut-tutted. 'The pier's shut, too. But everything will re-open once the oil's cleared.' They were still busy talking when the pub came into view.

None of them noticed the grey car keeping a discreet distance behind.

At a table in the pub garden, the youngsters chose food from a menu – steak-and-kidney pies with chips and peas. Susan also wanted a strawberry ice cream, Gary fancied a lemonade. Jenkins entered The Lobster Pot and gave their orders to a waitress.

Then, as casually as he could, the investigator began to search for Donovan. The bar was crowded. Jenkins' eyes flicked from person to person. No one here matched the caller's description. Was this a hoax? If so, not funny. Where *are* you, Donovan? Jenkins decided to check the other rooms.

Outside, Susan's mouth watered as lunch arrived. Gary reached for the tomato ketchup. They didn't speak until their plates were clean.

Meanwhile, the investigator had completed his search. No Donovan. Frowning, Jenkins pressed forward and managed to attract the barmaid's attention. He bought a drink. I'll give him ten more minutes, he thought.

In the garden, Gary and Susan felt full and content. Gary started to tell a joke. Suddenly, he was interrupted. A shadow fell across the table. They looked up.

'Hello, Susan . . .'

The voice was deep. Foreign? It belonged to the biggest man Susan had ever seen. He had a shock of hair, so blond it was almost white. The giant stranger smiled. Like a shark, thought Gary. Susan shuddered . . .

Inside the pub, Jenkins glanced at his watch, then beckoned the barmaid. Had she served anyone resembling Donovan?

'Now you mention it, I did. You just missed him, love. He left a few minutes before you came in. A couple of mates collected him. He didn't seem too keen on going at first, but they talked him into it.'

'Thanks.' The investigator's spine tingled. Mates, eh? Some mates! Would Donovan soon follow Larsen to the grave? Intercon had no conscience.

Jenkins felt as if he'd been punched in the

stomach. Susan! Why did I bring her? They'll stop at nothing . . .

He barged through the crowd and out into the garden.

The children were gone.

CHAPTER ELEVEN

Kidnap

'Hello, Susan . . .' The words had been friendly enough. But goose pimples rose on Susan's arms. Then the towering stranger smiled No, she didn't like him one bit. Who was he? How did he know her name? What did he want?

The blond giant bent down, resting a huge hand on her shoulder. Susan stared across the table at Gary in alarm. He moved his chair closer, rapidly scanning the pub garden. There was no one near.

'I'm Sven Ullman.' The big man tried another smile, again reminding Gary of a shark. 'Call me Sven. Your father will be busy for a while, Susan. So he asked me to take you – and Gary, of course – to the fair.'

Liar! Susan shouted in her head. The fair was closed, and her father knew it.

Gary's foot touched hers under the table.

'Thank you, Sven,' she said as sweetly as she could. 'But I just want to have a word with Dad first.'

Ullman's hand tightened on her shoulder. 'I told you – he's busy. Let's go now.'

Swivelling in his chair, Gary searched the garden for help. The nearest people, an old couple, were at the far end. He spotted a grey car with its engine revving, parked outside the pub. Behind the wheel sat a figure in a black leather jacket. The spy!

Susan said: 'Sven, I need to go to the lavatory.'

'You can wait till the fair.' Ullman's voice was hard.

Gary pretended to tie his shoe-lace. Ullman was

looking at the car. Seizing his chance, Gary whispered to Susan: 'When I say so, make a dash for it. To the right. I'll go left.'

Ullman's cruel gaze returned to them. Had he heard? He put his other hand on Gary's shoulder, and guided the children towards the car.

Suddenly, Gary stamped on the giant's foot, twisting as he did so. 'Now!' yelled Gary. Susan wriggled free, darting off. Gary broke into a sprint. Cursing, Ullman hobbled forward. The kids were escaping!

Then Susan tripped. Crashing headlong, she gasped with pain as gravel grazed her elbow. But almost immediately, she was up and running. Not soon enough, though. For, seeing Susan fall, the driver had leapt from the car. Now, he and Ullman were closing in.

Susan swerved, trying to zig-zag between them. If she could just get past the limping giant . . . As though reading Susan's thoughts, the black-jacketed driver cut across her path. She was cornered! Wide-eyed, Susan waited like a terrified rabbit. Ullman grabbed her sore elbow, which was bleeding slightly, and she cried out.

The sight of this stopped Gary in his tracks. He made no further attempt to get away. The driver pounced on him, snarling: 'One more stunt like that, sonny, and Ullman will break her arm!'

Roughly, he bundled Gary into the back seat of the car where Susan was already cowering beside the giant.

Seconds later, the car roared off – in the opposite direction to the fair.

A single glance confirmed Jenkins' worse fears: Susan and Gary weren't there. Rushing through the pub garden, he reached the road, peered both ways.

No sign of them. He wiped his damp brow as if trying to clear his brain. Think, man, think!

They wouldn't go off alone. Anyway, Susan would certainly have let him know. So the children must've gone with someone else. But Susan had left no message. Why? She couldn't . . .

Kidnap! The very word sickened him. Jenkins took a deep breath, forcing himself to face the facts. After all, he was supposed to be a trained investigator, wasn't he? Bitterly, he remembered the stolen photograph – a warning only a fool would have ignored.

Head down, Jenkins strode back towards The Lobster Pot. In the garden, he questioned the old man and woman who were just finishing their lunch.

Yes, they had seen the children. 'Playing a game with two men,' said the woman. 'But the little girl fell and hurt herself.'

A lump rose in Jenkins' throat. 'What happened then?' he asked huskily.

'The grown-ups took her and the boy to a car,' replied the woman. 'A grey car, it was.'

'When? Which way did they go?' Jenkins quickly extracted the answers.

Naturally, the old couple hadn't noticed the car's number. But the man gave quite a good description of the vehicle and its owners.

Jenkins surveyed the garden. No other witnesses. Now what? Contact Superintendent Compton, phone Aunt Maude – and Gary's father, Commander Izzard. Should he tell Joan yet? She'd never forgive him if anyone harmed their daughter. He'd never forgive himself. And what about poor Gary . . . ?

But another shock was looming. 'Scuse me, mister.' A freckle-faced boy thrust a brown envelope into the investigator's hand. Jenkins stared at him sharply. 'What's this?'

'Dunno, mister,' mumbled the boy. 'A guy on a motorbike said to give it you. Gave me a pound note.'

'Okay, lad. Thanks.'

Jenkins ripped open the envelope. Inside was a short note, printed in capitals. Jenkins' blood ran cold as he read: WE'VE GOT YOUR KID. IF YOU WANT HER TO STAY HEALTHY, KEEP THE COPS OUT OF IT. YOU'LL BE HEARING FROM US.

'Slow down!' bellowed Ullman. The grey car skidded crazily round a corner, missing a pillar box by inches. 'Want to kill us? Get us caught for speeding?' The driver grunted, and trod less heavily on the accelerator.

Gary and Susan had bumped heads when the car lurched sideways. They already ached from kneeling on the floor behind the front seats. But Ullman kept them there – 'so you can't see or be seen.'

Gary craned his neck and glared defiantly at the blond giant.

'Where are you taking us?'

'Shut up!'

'You won't get away with this. My father . . .'

'I said shut it, sonny!' Ullman wrenched Susan's bad arm. She whimpered. Gary didn't speak again.

The car was travelling more smoothly now. At about 40 mph, Gary estimated, glimpsing the tops of a row of trees beyond the window. This wasn't Southead, he felt sure.

Ullman and the driver – named Bert – began talking. 'That big mouth Larsen could've lost you and me a lot of money,' rumbled Ullman. 'So could

Donovan. Troublemakers! Still, they won't make any more trouble.'

Bert sniggered. 'No. Not unless you believe in ghosts. And we've got our hostages. Hadn't counted on the boy. But I s'pose two's better than one. Can't wait to get rid of 'em, though.'

Hearing this, Susan paled. *Get rid of*? What did he mean? Set them free? Or . . .

Gary sensed Susan's anxiety. Catching her eye, he put on his most confident grin. She succeeded in returning a tiny smile.

The car sped onwards, and the men's conversation petered out. Gary hoped he'd fooled Susan, but he couldn't fool himself. He was scared. Why hadn't he shouted for help in the garden? It might have worked. Too late now. They were captives. Ullman – was that the giant's real name? And the driver who looked like a weasel, was he really called Bert? Probably not, Gary guessed. They'd assume false identities. Unless . . . A chilling thought struck him. He and Susan had seen the men's faces, could identify them to the police. But the two thugs needn't worry about that if . . . Gary made himself think on . . . if they 'got rid of' their hostages.

The car swung left, bouncing and rocking over uneven ground. Susan slumped forward, wincing as she scraped her elbow. Ullman sneered when Gary dabbed the blood with a handkerchief. 'Serves her right for trying to run away.'

Gradually, the car slowed. Were they arriving? Where? What next?

'Pass me the blindfolds, Bert.' Ullman put a black cloth over Susan's eyes, tying it tightly at the back and clumsily pulling her hair. Before Gary was blindfolded, he checked his watch. Roughly twenty minutes since they left The Lobster Pot. So Southead couldn't be far.

'Out!' ordered Ullman. Awkwardly, with cramped legs, the young friends scrambled into the open. 'Stand still and listen.' They turned their heads in the direction of the voice. 'Right,' growled the invisible giant, 'I'll say this just once – while you're here, you'll do exactly as you're told. Always. You can't escape. But if you try, I'll make you wish you'd never been born.'

There was a pause, then Gary and Susan felt a vice-like grip on their necks. 'Understand, kiddies?' They said yes together. 'Okay, move!' Ullman shoved them from behind.

As he stumbled forward, Gary heard a familiar sound. Lapping water. The sea? Now he was climbing a springy slope. It creaked, must be wood . . . a gang plank! Soon he and Susan set foot on a swaying surface. Gary knew for certain they were aboard a boat. Someone guided them across the deck and down some steep steps.

'In there!' Bert's voice this time, followed by another push, the slam of a door and the click of a lock.

Gary tore off the blindfold. Blinking, he let his eyes adjust to the dim light of the cabin. 'You all right, Susan?'

'I will be when I can get this thing off. It's tangled in my hair.'

'Hold still.' Gingerly, Gary tried to untie the knot without hurting her. 'That's it.'

'Phew, thanks,' she breathed.

Gary walked over and tested the door. Locked, of course. Then, with Susan, he started to explore their prison. The daylight filtering through a small port-hole revealed two bunks, one above the other, in a corner of the brown-painted cabin. Gary tapped the wall – steel.

As he turned, his gaze was suddenly arrested. Another door! To his surprise, it opened when he twisted the handle. A way out? No such luck – just a poky room with a lavatory and wash-basin. A fragment of mirror, a grubby towel, a piece of soap, a metal bucket and a mop . . . nothing here to aid their getaway. Or was there?

While Susan washed her elbow under the tap, Gary undid the latch on the porthole. Gulls' cries and a salty sea smell floated into the cabin. Not too far away, beyond waves winking at the sun, land could be seen. This was an inlet – but where?

Peering down, Gary watched the sparkling water as it slapped the boat's side. A great day for sailing. Immediately, he squashed the thought. Forget about fun, Gary. Forget about everything except escape. What chance did he and Susan have? Almost none, he admitted miserably. And rescue? First, they must be found. Perhaps he could signal with the mirror or send a message in a bottle. Some hope!Tricks like that only paid off in adventure stories.

'Gary . . .' He looked round. Susan was sitting on the lower bunk.

'How's your arm?' he asked.

'I'll live.' Susan managed a smile. 'Look, I'm sorry for what's happened. It's all my fault.'

'Your fault? Don't be daft.'

'Those pigs were after *me*, not you. Didn't you hear them in the car?'

'Listen, Susan. We're friends, right?'

She nodded.

'Okay. Se we're in this together, and we'll get out of it together.'

'You're nice,' said Susan.

Gary scratched his ear. 'Not bad yourself,' he mumbled. 'Now, let's think about getting free.'

In the neighbouring cabin, Ullman stretched his huge frame on a bunk and belched. Empty beer cans littered the floor. He rolled over to face Bert, who sprawled in a chair studying the sports page of a newspaper. 'Better ditch the car tonight, Bert. Somewhere safe.'

'Yeah,' grunted the smaller man. 'Then all we've got to do is lie low till we move. Plenty of booze and grub on board.'

The giant yawned. 'Talking of food, where are the sandwiches we ordered? Don't trust that shifty sailor.'

Bert drew a gun from his jacket pocket and patted the barrel. 'He'll behave . . . or else! I'm a crack shot – as the cops'll find if they get too close.'

Ullman frowned. 'Cool it! There'll be enough corpses before this job is through.'

The weasel pocketed his gun. 'When we've had our grub, I'll pay a visit to those brats next door.'

Meanwhile, Susan sat staring gloomily into space. She had even less idea of how to escape than Gary. At last, she sighed: 'Why are we here?'

Gary moved away from the porthole. 'My guess is your father's found out something about *Saracen*, something Mercouri and his mob want kept quiet. They kidnapped us so your dad wouldn't talk.'

'What'll they do to us?'

'Nothing – they're just bluffing.' Like me, thought Gary. 'Prob'ly let us go soon.'

'But what if they don't?' Susan's blue eyes fixed him.

'The police'll save us. My dad and yours will see to that.'

'Really think so, Gary?'

He avoided her gaze, turning again to the porthole. Telling lies, even white ones, made him feel guilty. 'Sure. Bet you a month's pocket money.'

This time, the view of the inlet stirred a vague memory in Gary's mind. *Hadn't* he visited the place before? With Snuff, as a puppy?

At the thought of his dog, Gary suddenly needed to blow his nose. He fumbled for his handkerchief. Strange, he couldn't find it. He'd used it for Susan's elbow in the car, must've lost it later. Pity – his father had given him that handkerchief with the initial G embroidered in blue.

Sniffing, Gary clambered up to the top bunk and lay back, hands behind his head. Nothing to do now but wait – and keep their fingers crossed. A faint buzz of conversation came from the next cabin. Gary pressed his ear to the wall. If only he could hear the words . . .

Then he noticed a ventilator, above him. Jerking upright, he reached into his pocket and pulled out a Scout's knife. Luckily, the two bullies had been so sure of themselves that they hadn't bothered to search a mere kid.

Shakily, Gary opened the knife and began to unscrew the ventilator grille.

Susan's head appeared over the edge of the bunk. 'What on earth are you doing?'

Startled, Gary dropped the knife. 'Quiet!' he hissed. 'I want to eavesdrop on the enemy.'

Soon Gary had undone the last of the screws. He laid them on the blanket and, very carefully, took off the grille. Voices, much clearer now. It was almost like being next door. Gary licked his lips, hardly daring to breathe.

Ullman's gruff tones: 'Relax, Bert. In a week we'll be out of the country. By then, Intercon will own all the best property along the coast. Sold cheap by a bunch of mugs who've been conned – with the help of "respectable" English businessmen.'

Gary's eyes grew rounder.

A guffaw from Bert. 'What a joke! But why's Intercon in such a hurry?'

'The oil's being cleared faster than expected,' replied Ullman. 'Then there's the cops and that ruddy investigator. They may be wise to the main plan.'

Silence, followed by the clink of glasses.

'How long before we get the radio call, Sven?'

'A few hours. Relax, I tell you. Let's drink to Mercouri. A loony. But he's gonna make our fortunes. Lucky for us he'd do anything to get even with *Olympus*'s captain.'

Gary kept his ear glued to the ventilator, although the men had stopped talking. What else would they say? He heard the sound of movement . . .

Not long after, without warning, the door of the children's cabin was flung open. Bert! His glowering glance flew straight to the top bunk . . . and Gary, crouching by the black square where the ventilator grille had been.

'Come 'ere, snotty kid! I'll teach yer to listen in.'

Susan started to tremble. 'No . . . no . . . please don't . . .'

Bert lunged at Gary, catching him by the throat.

'Know what this is, sonny?'

Gary felt the cold, hard barrel of a gun against his ear. The thug spat. 'Say goodbye to your little girlfriend.'

Susan burst into tears.

CHAPTER TWELVE

Break-out

Sobbing, Susan buried her face in a blanket as the cabin door clanged shut. Gary . . . Gone . . . Marched off at gunpoint! She couldn't stop the tears. He'd been so brave, telling her she'd soon be safe. Not a word about what lay ahead for him. Poor Gary! Her friend. Sobs shook her until she felt weak.

At last, the crying subsided. Susan crawled off the bunk and shuffled to the tap to wash her face. The broken mirror reflected her despair.

Numbly, she returned to the bunk. She noticed Gary's knife lying where he'd left it. Suddenly, anger flushed her cheeks. Why hadn't she stabbed Bert? She would if she got another chance. Meanwhile, she slipped the knife under the blanket.

Sitting down, Susan held her head. What could she do? She wanted to ask Gary. Only then did the awful truth begin to dawn – her friend was gone for ever. Fresh tears welled in Susan's eyes. Shocked and heart-broken, she curled up on the bunk.

Crack!

Susan jumped. A shot?

They've killed Gary! She rushed across the cabin. Yelling at the top of her voice, she kicked and pounded the door.

But it was a long time before anyone came.

The sound of a key turning made Susan step back. A man she didn't recognize entered with a tray, which he put on the bottom bunk. He was small and skinny.

'Pig!' Susan sprang at him. 'You're all murderers. I hate you!'

The man raised his arm to ward off the blows.

'You barmy? Belt up and eat your grub.'

Susan thought of reaching for the knife, but decided against it – that was reserved for Bert. She continued calling the sailor names, blaming him for Gary's death. He seemed puzzled.

'Dunno what you're on about. I was just told to bring you some food. And I've gotta snip off a bit of your hair. Don't ask me why.'

Susan half believed him – maybe he didn't know what had happened to Gary. To her surprise, she submitted meekly when the man cut off a blonde lock with a pair of scissors. Stuffing the hair into his shirt pocket, he left.

Despite everything, Susan was ravenous. Using a spoon, she quickly emptied the plate of stew. She made short work, too, of a can of fizzy orangeade. Afterwards, she stretched out and slept.

A while later, she woke with a start. The cabin door was open. Ullman's vast bulk blocked the view. Stooping, the surly giant lurched forward. Susan shivered.

'Got a present for you, brat.' Ullman reached behind him. 'Not that you deserve it.'

With one powerful movement, he heaved a body on to the floor at Susan's feet.

'Gary!' As Susan bent down, the door slammed.

Silence. Then a groan. Gary sat up.

'You're alive!' Susan struggled between laughter and tears.

'Course I am.' Gary grinned, rubbing his knee.

'Oh, oh . . . thank goodness!' Susan flung her arms round his neck and kissed him.

'Steady on.'

Susan squatted, smiling. Questions poured from her. How had he escaped? Was he hurt? What about the shot?

'Whoa, one at a time.' Gary lifted a grubby hand and started to tell the story.

With a gun at his head, he'd thought he was a gonner. After leaving the cabin, Gary was forced to climb the stairs and cross the deck to the boat's bow. There Bert halted, gloating. Gary was given a lecture, full of swear words and punctuated by jabs to his stomach with the gun. Eventually, Bert finished. He had aimed the gun between Gary's eyes.

'That's when Ullman turned up,' Gary explained. 'Never thought I'd be glad to see *him*. Anyway, he hollered at Bert. The weasel didn't want to listen. But Ullman twisted his wrist – and the gun went off. Just missed me.'

'Cor!' Susan's jaw gaped. 'What happened next, Gary? And why were you so long?'

'Nothing much. Ullman kept the gun, and Bert slunk away to sulk. Then Bert came back and told him I'd been eavesdropping. Ullman was really wild. Said *he'd* shoot me if I stepped out of line again.'

Susan sucked in her breath. 'Better be careful, Gary.'

'I will, don't worry.'

He went on to finish the story. The giant had seized Gary's ear, dragging him up and down the deck and shouting. In the end – 'probably because he was tired of walking' – Ullman hauled Gary back to the cabin.

'And here I am,' he concluded. 'A bit sore, but still in one piece.'

Susan gazed at him admiringly. 'A hero.'

Gary awarded himself an imaginary medal and grinned.

'Tell you what, Susan. I found out quite a lot about this boat. She's a big motor cruiser, called *Scorpion*. Pretty fast, I'd guess, and she's got up-to-date radar and radio. Might come in handy, that information.'

Susan couldn't see how, but she nodded.

Then she remembered the knife. Gary's eyes glinted as she passed it over. He'd find a good use for it.

His gaze fell on Susan's empty plate. 'I could eat a horse,' he sighed. 'Bet I don't get any food.'

But Gary was in luck. Soon after, the cabin door swung open and the sailor brought in a meal. Gary swallowed the stew in record time.

Sipping his drink, he watched the man screw the ventilator grille into place. A bunch of keys dangled from his belt. Could Gary snatch them? He fingered the knife in his jeans' pocket. No, the break-out had to be planned.

The crewman locked the door behind him. Susan yawned, which set Gary off, and suddenly they both realized they were exhausted.

'Sleep now,' murmured Gary. Susan's head drooped.

Beyond the porthole, a bright star shone. It must be late.

Gary climbed up to the top bunk and flopped out.

'G'night, Susan.'

'Goodnight, Gary.' In the bunk below, Susan smiled. Thank heavens her friend was safe and sound! Without him, she'd have been scared stiff.

Gary's thoughts were more sombre. He had escaped death – just. But could he and Susan escape from the cruiser? A feeling of dread crept over him. Would tomorrow be even worse?

* * *

LAY OFF, SNOOPER. TELL REGAL TO PAY THE SARACEN CLAIM AT ONCE. NO COPS – OR YOU'LL NEVER SEE YOUR PRETTY DAUGHTER AGAIN.

A lock of blonde hair was stuck to the ransom note. Jenkins' legs turned to jelly. He sat down heavily.

£42 million for Susan's life: that's what they were demanding. A fantastic price. Jenkins would have died to save his daughter, but should he let Intercon get away with robbery? Besides, the police were already involved. Jenkins had reported the kidnapping – the latest in a list of Intercon crimes which included murder. He couldn't back out now.

With an unsteady hand, the investigator lit a cigarette. He re-read the brutal note, and began pacing his hotel room. Perhaps Regal could stall for time until the kidnappers were caught. Or maybe the insurance company could pay the money, then get it back when Intercon's bosses were brought to trial . . . if they ever were.

Stop kidding yourself, Jenkins. He sank into a chair, fondling the blonde lock. On the table beside him lay another envelope. He opened it, guessing the contents. A typed statement, signed by the salvage ship's captain, confirmed that *Saracen* was an old hulk. The final proof of fraud – but it gave Jenkins no satisfaction now. He wished he'd never heard the name *Saracen*.

And how was he going to break the terrible news to Joan? He blamed himself for the kidnap. If he'd been less careless, Susan might still be free.

Feeling sick, Jenkins picked up the phone to call Superintendent Compton.

Brr, brr . . . brr, brr . . . Mrs Izzard grabbed the

receiver. 'Yes?' She sounded desperate. 'You want to speak to my husband . . . About *Gary* . . . What? . . . All right . . . David!'

Commander Izzard almost ran to the phone, a plain-clothes police sergeant with him.

'Izzard here.'

'Don't talk – just listen,' said a muffled voice. 'Too bad your boy's caught up in this. But you asked for it by blabbing in court. Anyhow, he's our prisoner. Make sure the insurance investigator follows instructions. Otherwise the kid's had it – '

The Commander broke in. 'If you hurt Gary, I'll . . .'

'You'll do as you're told, Izzard. And nothing else.'

'Wait a minute, man!'

'Think I'm stupid? Your phone's probably tapped. Just get Jenkins to co-operate – or you'll be minus a son.'

The line went dead.

At Southead police station, Superintendent Compton pulled a sympathetic face as though John Jenkins could see him at the other end of the phone. He knew Jenkins must be going through hell. The bald policeman respected the Regal Investigator – they were both first-class professionals – and he was more worried than he would admit about the girl's kidnap. Grimly, Compton noted down the terms of the ransom demand.

The superintendent spoke gently: 'We're doing everything we can, Mr Jenkins. We've circulated descriptions of the children, the kidnappers and the car to police forces around the country. And my men are conducting a full-scale search of the area. No leads yet – but I'm confident we'll find your daughter. Try to stay calm.'

'I *am* trying,' muttered Jenkins.

'By the way,' added Compton, 'there's been some progress on the property case. But I don't suppose you care much at the moment.'

'You're right,' agreed Jenkins. 'I don't give a damn. Bring my daughter back to me, Superintendent. Then I'll help you stamp out the whole rotten racket.'

The insurance investigator hung up. Minutes later, he hurried from the hotel. Perhaps *he* could find Susan . . .

Aboard the cruiser, in their cabin prison, Susan was the first to stir. Was it the sunlight streaming through the porthole that had woken her? Or the throbbing of *Scorpion*'s engine? She couldn't say. But she knew one thing: the boat was moving.

Rolling off her bunk, Susan padded barefoot to the porthole and peered out. *Scorpion* was slicing the water, which fell back in foamy folds. Beyond, land slid by – so near and yet it might as well be a thousand miles away. Susan could see a lone hiker striding along in the fresh and sunny morning air. She'd give anything to swop places with him . . . provided Gary was free, too.

She glanced over her shoulder at the top bunk. Soft snores rose from Gary's sleeping form. Should she wake him? Susan hesitated, then lightly touched his arm. Gary stretched, sat up and grinned drowsily.

'Morning, Susan.' He swung his legs over the edge of the bunk.

Suddenly, he was alert – this was no day for dawdling.

While Susan washed, Gary took her place at the porthole. Where was the cruiser heading? Would escape be harder than ever? But even as he pondered, the engine note changed, fading to a faint thrum. Abruptly, the noise ceased. Then he heard a splash. Craning, Gary saw the anchor rope tauten, felt *Scorpion* jerk like a tethered horse. They were moored in the middle of the inlet.

Susan returned, hastily drying her face. 'Gary!' she cried. 'Look – a boat.'

He almost pushed her aside. A dinghy, powered by an outboard motor, was slanting away from *Scorpion*. Ullman steered, while Bert sat uneasily in the bobbing bow.

Going where? Gary's mind got busy. A rendezvous with their leader? The two thugs were dimwits – otherwise they'd have confiscated his knife – so they wouldn't act without orders. And hadn't they mentioned a radio call?

Susan was thinking, too, but not of the dinghy. What's Dad doing? she wondered. In fact, at that very moment, her father was on board a launch speeding towards Southead traffic control room where he and Commander Izzard would join forces in an all-out attempt to rescue the children.

'Now's our chance!' There was excitement in Gary's voice.

Susan stared at him blankly.

'I've got a plan.' He quickly outlined it.

She shook her head doubtfully. 'It wouldn't work, Gary. We'd never get away with it.'

Gary looked disappointed, then stubborn. 'You got any better ideas?'

'No, but . . .'

'We must try, Susan. It's our only hope.'

Several seconds passed before she said, smiling: 'Okay. After all, you *were* right about the spy.'

'Good. I knew you wouldn't let me down.'

A piercing scream echoed round the cabin. On

deck, the sailor dropped the rope he was coiling. What the . . . Perishing kids! Another scream. Up to their tricks, are they? I'll soon put a stop to that. But by the time he'd reached the foot of the stairs, the crewman was more concerned than annoyed. Maybe the youngsters really were in trouble . . .

A third scream greeting him as he approached the cabin. He fumbled in his haste to unlock the door. Gary rushed forward, clutching the man's arm. 'It's Susan . . . pain . . . her stomach!' The sailor moved rapidly to the lower bunk where Susan gasped and moaned. He leant down.

Clang!

The metal bucket hit his head hard. The sailor slumped to his knees, striking his head on a corner of the bunk, and fell sideways. For a moment, Gary panicked. I've killed him! No, the man was breathing, just stunned. Later, Gary would feel guilty. But now, he had other things on his mind.

'I've got the keys, Susan. Let's go.'

'Shouldn't we tie him up and gag him? We could use the blindfolds.'

'No need. No time, anyway. Come on!'

The crewman stirred. His eyelids twitched. He seemed to be seeing double – four children were leaving the cabin. He heard a click as he was locked in with his own key.

Gary set off briskly along the corridor, Susan following on legs that were stiff from lack of exercise. Up the steps and out on to the deck. She bumped into him when he stopped suddenly, dazzled by the sunlight. Shading his eyes, he turned to her and grinned. 'Told you it would work!'

Susan's expression showed she could hardly believe their luck. Gary left her and began a swift inspection of the deck. Ullman and Bert had taken the only dinghy. Lifebelts? Gary couldn't find any. No life-jackets either. And he'd never be able to start and steer *Scorpion*. Gary rejoined Susan.

'We'll have to swim ashore,' he said. 'Not far.'

Susan gulped. 'But . . . I can't swim!'

Gary's face clouded. He looked almost angry. 'Oh, no.' Then he brightened. 'That's okay – I'll tow you. I've got a certificate for lifesaving.'

Susan was close to tears. 'It's no good, Gary. I'm scared of the water. I just can't . . .'

'But it's easy. Nothing to it. I won't let you drown.'

Susan hung her head. 'Too frightened,' she whispered. 'I'm useless. I've ruined everything.'

Gary reached out and squeezed her arm. Susan looked up. '*You* go . . . fetch help. Leave me here.'

'Don't talk tripe. I'm not going without you.'

They stood in silence. The escape plan had failed. Susan started to say sorry, but Gary interrupted. 'The radio!' he exclaimed. 'Of course!'

With his arm round Susan's shoulders, he scurried to the cockpit which housed the radio. Soon, watched by Susan, he was tuning the complicated-looking equipment to the right frequency. He'd learnt a lot from his visits to Southead traffic control room.

Less than a minute later, Gary was speaking to Lieutenant Mitchell. The astonished young officer handed him over to Commander Izzard double quick.

'Gary! Thank God! Where are you, son? Are you hurt?'

The boy was calmer than his father as he answered the questions. Wasting no time, he reported the key facts: *Scorpion* was moored in an inlet about twenty minutes' drive from The Lobster Pot. Gary couldn't identify the location, but he thought he'd been there once before with Snuff. He described the kidnappers, mentioning that they were armed and dangerous.

While Gary talked, Lieutenant Mitchell tried to get a radio fix to pinpoint the cruiser's position.

Then John Jenkins' voice came through the loudspeaker. Susan nearly choked. 'Dad!' Gary left them to their conversation, and explored the cockpit. In a corner was a yellow box. He lifted the lid – life-jackets! Surely Susan would brave the water if she was wearing one of those . . .

Gary took over at the radio. Briefly, he repeated what he'd overheard the crooks say – including remarks about Intercon's property swindle. It didn't all make sense to Gary, but it did to Jenkins. And it certainly would to the police.

Suddenly, Susan squeaked. 'Listen!'

Gary swivelled, straining his ears. *Putt . . . putt . . . putt* . . . An outboard motor! Ullman and Bert? He poked his head round the door. A long way off he spotted a dinghy. The thugs were coming back!

CHAPTER THIRTEEN

Intercon

In the control room, Commander Izzard fought to keep his voice steady. Gripping the radio microphone, he said: 'Don't panic, Gary. We'll get you both out of this . . .'

There was a crackle on the receiver. 'Gary . . . can you hear me, son?' No answer.

Izzard met Jenkins' gaze and saw a desperation that matched his own. The investigator turned away to hide his thoughts. Susan! So plucky, yet she must be terrified. Gary, too. Trapped by a pair of . . . killers.

'Mitchell!' Commander Izzard cut into the silence. 'Did you locate *Scorpion*?'

'I tried to, sir.'

'Tried?'

'Kept losing the signal. Nearest I can get is that she's some way east of us. I'm sorry.'

'Save it, Lieutenant.' Izzard's mouth was a thin, hard line. 'Pass me the map.'

Mitchell almost jumped to obey.

The Commander began muttering to himself: '20 minutes from The Lobster Pot. That puts the cruiser within 15 miles of the pub.' He drew a circle on the map with a geometrical compass. 'And Mitchell says she's to the east . . .'

Meanwhile, Jenkins phoned Southead police station, relaying Gary's information. Then he joined Izzard at the chart table. 'I'll organize a helicopter search,' declared the Commander. 'Let's pray those apes on *Scorpion* mistake the choppers for part of the oil-fighting force.'

The two men exchanged a sympathetic glance, each knowing how the other felt.

Jenkins wiped his sweating palms on a handkerchief, and returned to the telephone. Now came a task he'd been dreading. But it had to be done – he couldn't delay telling Joan any longer. Better she should learn about the kidnapping from him than from a television bulletin.

As events turned out, that day's TV broadcasts didn't mention the children's disappearance. The police had succeeded in keeping it quiet. What news there was of the collision's aftermath was all encouraging. Cameras showed beaches nearly restored to their former state – largely because *Olympus* was no longer spewing oil. The injured diver, now recovered, posed for photographers outside Southead General Hospital. Tourists were told they needn't cancel their holiday bookings. On harbour quays, trawlermen pointed to improving catches. And at rescue stations, RSPB officers happily reported that the flood of crippled sea birds had dwindled to a trickle.

Jenkins could know none of this as he dialled his home. In any case, he wouldn't have cared. Only one thing mattered to him – what was happening aboard *Scorpion*.

Putt . . . putt . . . putt. The crooks' dinghy nosed nearer and nearer. Abandoning the radio, Gary hissed: 'Get down . . . out of sight!' Susan ducked fast, and crawled towards him across the floor of the cruiser's cockpit. Her eyes were round with fear.

'They'll do something terrible to us, Gary.'

'Shh!' Cautiously, Gary peered round the edge of the door. The dinghy was still a few hundred yards away. 'Keep your head low and follow me!' he whispered urgently.

Before Susan had time to think, she found herself copying Gary's crouching run as he scampered to the stairs and plunged down them. Panting, she caught him up outside their cabin door. Gary unlocked it with the stolen key, and pulled her inside.

The imprisoned crewman goggled. Forgetting his aching head, he leapt up from the bunk and charged at Gary. 'Gotcha, rotten kid! I've a good mind to knock your block off.'

Gary winced, his arm clamped in a bony grip.

Understandably, the sailor was furious. He looked as though he meant to carry out his threat. But Susan's words made him step back.

'They're coming – Ullman and Bert!'

'What?' Alarm registered on the crewman's face. 'Oh Gawd! If they find I let you get out, they'll kill me.'

Gary broke in. 'They needn't know. *We* won't say anything if *you* don't.'

The man's expression was almost comical. 'You mean . . .'

'Lock us up,' finished Susan. 'Pretend nothing's happened. But be quick!'

Just then, something bumped *Scorpion*'s side. The dinghy? An impatient shout from Ullman answered the question.

'Hurry!' urged Gary, handing over the bunch of keys.

The sailor dithered for a moment, mumbled his thanks and dived for the door.

'Remember,' Susan called after him, 'not a word!'

The door lock clicked, and the children heard the sound of running feet.

Suddenly, Susan bent double. Gary looked at her

anxiously. But it was only an attack of the giggles, relief after all they'd been through.

Gary crossed to the porthole and gazed out moodily. Still prisoners! But at least he'd managed to contact his father – and the thugs didn't know that. Nor did the sailor. So even if the man decided to tell tales, he couldn't sneak about the radio.

Then an unpleasant thought struck Gary. Supposing Ullman or Bert had spotted the two figures dashing from the cockpit . . .

Some 3,500 miles away, in the Arab state of Kuwait, a cavalcade of limousines glided up to a big white building. The temperature outside Intercon headquarters was a baking 49 degrees Centigrade – 120 degrees Fahrenheit – and in the surrounding desert it was even hotter. There, the scattered oil wells which made Kuwait so rich were hidden by sand storms.

Alighting from their chauffeur-driven cars, men of a dozen different nationalities hastened inside the air-conditioned building. Intercon's top operators had flown in to Kuwait from around the world for an emergency meeting – and they could hardly wait to leave this parched place where even the trees had to be imported and kept watered.

A uniformed attendant led the visitors through a cool, marble-panelled entrance hall to the board room.

'Wonder what the Director wants,' murmured an American to the Frenchman walking beside him. 'Must be important . . .' The Frenchman seemed tense. 'We'll soon find out.'

Abdul Hussein, chief of Intercon, sat at the head of a long polished table with high-backed chairs on either side. Above him hung his portrait in oils, a flattering picture which showed a handsome, dignified figure in full Arab dress. But today, he wore a white suit and black silk shirt. His yellow tie, also silk, was secured by a diamond pin. He was wearing dark glasses.

'Welcome, gentlemen,' purred the Director. Like everyone there, he spoke fluent English. Hussein grinned broadly. 'Please be seated.'

Quietly, Intercon's senior managers took their seats, marked by name cards on the table in front of them. They weren't deceived by Hussein's soft voice and flashing smile. Behind his dark glasses, they knew, lurked crocodile eyes.

Turning his head slowly, the Director looked from face to face. The other men felt uneasy – as if he could read their minds. At last, Hussein leant forward.

'I have summoned you here,' he began, 'to discuss Intercon's future and yours. As you know, this is one of the world's biggest companies. I intend it to become *the* biggest. Oil, ships, property . . . we are expanding everywhere. Nothing and nobody can stop us now.'

The Director paused, glancing round the table. Several of the managers nodded their agreement eagerly.

'Recently,' Hussein continued, 'we have set our sights on the south coast of England. I devised the master-plan myself. It involved an old Intercon vessel, due to be scrapped, colliding with a super-tanker in the English Channel. Many thousands of tons of crude oil spilt into the sea, then on to the shore. So sad!'

A ripple of laughter ran through the room, the last there would be at that meeting.

Hussein allowed himself a brief smile before adding: 'A clever scheme, yes? With the beaches unusable and no tourists, seaside businesses will be forced to sell up. And we can buy – at rock-bottom prices.'

The loss of *Olympus* and its cargo had damaged a rival company, Hussein pointed out. It was also punishment for Captain Duncan Farrar, an ex-Intercon employee with the 'dangerous' habit of being honest.

'A perfect strategy,' sighed the Director. He fell silent. Then he began to twist the ruby ring on his left hand – an ominous sign to those who knew him.

'Perfect!' he repeated. But this time, he was shouting. His fist crashed down on the polished wood, sending a glass of iced water flying.

'So why was it changed? Why did you' – he jabbed the Frenchman sitting by him – 'disobey my orders? Your stupidity and greed may have ruined the whole project!'

A choking sound came from the Frenchman. 'I . . . I . . .'

Hussein rose to his feet. 'Imbecile! Lost your tongue? Well, you'd better find it. Meanwhile, I shall explain why your services are no longer required.'

The Director smoothed his sleek black hair. A deep hush descended on the room.

Ignoring the Frenchman, Hussein addressed the other managers. His tone was calm and very cold. 'This blockhead Dupont claimed £42 million insurance for the sunk Intercon ship. An old tub – yet he tried to pretend it was one of our newest tankers loaded with valuable oil. The insurance company – Regal – sent out an investigator. And that's when the trouble started.'

Hussein went on to tell how Jenkins had uncovered the feeble fraud, aided by a pair of talkative crew members – both since eliminated. 'Then, to make matters worse, Dupont's goons kidnapped two children. If the police connect Intercon with these crimes . . .'

The Director took off his dark glasses and stared at Dupont until his blubbery jowls shook. 'Did you think I wouldn't discover your treachery? Greedy fool! You have jeopardized a property deal worth billions of pounds.'

Again, the Frenchman struggled to speak. Hussein waved him aside and continued his grim lecture. The collision was supposed to occur at night, he said, further out to sea. But *Olympus* sank in shallower water . . . divers were able to seal the wreck before all the oil leaked out . . . they had also got a good look at the so-called tanker *Saracen*. And the bugging device – it should have been removed soon after the crash, not left for some frogman to find . . .

'In fact, Dupont, you and your friends bungled everything. You will *all* pay dearly.'

Hussein sat down. There was a stir around the table. The Frenchman cleared his throat. 'It wasn't my fault, Mr Hussein. The captain – Mercouri, he's the one. Wanted more money, couldn't control him, crazy for revenge on Farrar. And nobody expected the crew to talk. The officers were well bribed, and most of the sailors didn't know what was going on. Those who guessed were blackmailed to keep their mouths shut.'

The Director smiled, opened a gold case and took out a king-size cigarette. Three men offered their lighters, but Hussein lit it himself.

Dupont relaxed a little. He sounded almost confident as he added: 'Anyway, Mr Hussein – Abdul – I meant to give Intercon the insurance money. I thought you'd be pleased.'

Hussein tapped the ash from his cigarette. Softly, he said: 'You're a liar, Dupont. I'll show no mercy.'

He slid his hand under the table, pressing a buzzer. Almost immediately, two huge attendants entered the room.

Witho. looking up, Hussein murmured: 'Mr Dupont will be leaving us . . . for good.'

The blood drained from the Frenchman's face. He didn't bother to argue or protest. He was doomed – and he knew it.

Dupont and his escorts departed. It was half a minute before Hussein spoke. 'Most unfortunate,' he sighed. 'If only Dupont had remained loyal . . . I'm sure I can rely on *you*, gentlemen.'

Suddenly, the red phone in front of him shrilled. The call he was expecting? He checked his watch – 2.30, three hours ahead of English time. Hussein lifted the receiver, identified himself, listened, fired several questions. A pause. 'Good.' He hung up.

Briskly, he passed on the news fiom England. 'We must move fast. The pollution is being cleared. But it seems the police don't know about our property project.'

However, Hussein warned, Intercon's managers in every country should be on the lookout for snoopers.

Then he turned to the German beside him. 'Schmidt, you take over from Dupont. My personal jet will fly you to England. Your first job: see that Mercouri and the crew are shipped out at once.'

Schmidt was moving towards the door when Hussein called him back. 'One more thing. Those children . . . dispose of them.'

CHAPTER FOURTEEN

The Chase

Commander Izzard crouched as the black springer spaniel bounded up to him. 'What is it, Snuff? What've you found?'

Snuff whined, pawing the Commander's knee and quivering with excitement. The dog opened his mouth and let go of what he was carrying. A white rag? No, not a rag, Izzard soon saw. A handkerchief, grimy and blood-stained. He laid it on the ground. Snuff pawed him again, as if trying to tell him something. Izzard straightened the crumpled linen square . . . then noticed the G embroidered in blue on one corner. Snuff's nose had made no mistake. The handkerchief belonged to Gary!

'Good boy! Clever boy!' Commander Izzard patted the dog's head.

So they'd come to the right place. This *was* the inlet. Izzard had suspected it when he spotted the car tracks and the marks that could have been made by a gang plank at the water's edge. Now he knew.

The Commander raised his powerful Navy binoculars. Adjusting the focus, he scanned the expanse of small waves, sequinned by sunlight. No sign of the moored cruiser. Izzard's heart sank. Where is she? He searched further out, towards the open sea. Nothing. Despairingly, he started to lower the glasses . . . Wait! What's that? He peered through the lenses. Yes, the gleam of brass, a polished rail above the stern of a boat . . . heading for the Channel.

The name – could he read it? Straining his eyes,

he deciphered the swaying letters one by one. S . . . C . . . O . . . R . . . P . . . I . . . O . . . N. *Scorpion*!

Ullman lolled on the cruiser's deck, drinking beer and throwing the empty cans overboard. Bert, looking slightly green, clung to the rail as *Scorpion* hit choppier water. Behind them, the sailor steered.

'Dunno why we've gotta leave,' complained Bert. 'It was comfortable here.'

'Orders,' rumbled Ullman. 'Go to Southead. Collect Mercouri. We just do as we're told.'

'But . . . Southead!' The weasel went a deeper shade of green. 'Dead risky. Place'll be crawling with cops.'

Ullman shrugged. 'What if it is? We'll be safe enough in a crowded port. And the law's got no reason to think this isn't a pleasure boat.'

'I still don't like it, Sven.'

The blond giant snorted. 'Stop worrying. Remember the money. Besides, the boss knows what he's doing. Dupont's smarter than any dumb cop . . .'

In the cockpit, the sailor shifted the wheel to starboard. *Scorpion* heeled. Glancing at the barometer, he noted that the pressure had fallen. Dirty weather on the way? That's all I need! Clouds now hid the sun, and a freshening wind snatched and scattered spray from the rising waves.

The crewman's nerves were frayed. He couldn't forget the narrow squeak he'd had when the thugs returned in the dinghy. Lucky for me they don't know the kids got out! He rubbed the lump on the back of his head. Brats! Even so, he felt sorry for them. Poor little perishers – I wouldn't want to be in their shoes . . .

Below deck, Susan lay on her bunk feeling sick. Gary steadied himself against the wall, watching the wild water leap at the porthole. The escape attempt had remained a secret, he reasoned, otherwise Ullman or Bert would have burst into the cabin hours ago. Gary was grateful for that. But gloomy thoughts haunted him. Bert's words – 'get rid of' – kept echoing in the boy's mind. Unless rescue came soon, it might be too late . . .

Pocketing the handkerchief, Commander Izzard sprinted to his car. Snuff followed, swiftly overtaking him. Izzard wrenched open the door on the driver's side. Snuff jumped in, scrabbling to the passenger seat. Seconds later, the car surged forward, showering stones from the spinning back wheels.

The nearest phone box was three quarters of a mile away. Izzard gritted his teeth as the speeding car juddered over bumpy ground. At last – the road! Swinging right, with Snuff slithering to the floor, Izzard accelerated hard. Soon the phone box was in view.

But vandals had been there first. The apparatus was useless. 'Damn them!' Izzard left the box. There was a house opposite. He dashed across the road and up the garden path. After what seemed an age, a young woman carrying a baby answered the door. 'Emergency!' panted the Commander. 'Your phone.'

Within a minute, he had reported *Scorpion*'s whereabouts to the police. Next, he contacted Southead traffic control room. 'Mitchell, I've located the cruiser. She's putting out to sea from Cormorant Inlet. Lay on a helicopter to shadow her. But for God's sake, tell the pilot to be careful . . .'

In Superintendent Compton's office, John Jenkins sat staring into space. He hardly heard when the senior policeman confided: 'We're ready to close our net on the local sharks behind the property swindle.'

Jenkins nodded. 'Good,' he murmured vaguely. But all he could think of was Susan. Sensing this, Compton stopped talking.

A sergeant entered, passed over a written message and left. The superintendent read it out.

Jenkins slopped hot coffee on his hand and nearly dropped the cup. *Scorpion* sighted! The hunt was moving in. He grinned at Compton. 'Not long now, eh?' The superintendent smiled half-heartedly, reluctant to puncture Jenkins' soaring hopes.

Gravely, Compton said: 'Capturing *Scorpion* should be simple, but getting the children off safely . . .'

The cruiser wallowed in a heavy swell. Gary pulled the blanket from his bunk and spread it over Susan. Twice, she'd had to get up and stagger to the lavatory to be sick. Gary gazed down sympathetically. 'Wish I could help you. I know how rotten it feels.'

Susan moaned. 'I think I'm dying.'

Without meaning to be unkind, Gary laughed. 'Rubbish! Once you're on dry land again, you won't even remember being seasick.'

Susan closed her eyes and said nothing.

Dry land . . . the thought of it set Gary yearning. Would he ever be free? Free to do the things he'd always taken for granted – like going for a walk with Snuff? He touched the knife in his pocket. Maybe escape was still possible . . .

On deck, Bert was bent double, head dangled above the writhing water. Very slowly, he eased himself upright. Ullman regarded him indifferently. 'Wait till the weather's really rough . . .'

Holding his stomach, Bert turned back to the rail. But suddenly he froze. 'Sven!' He pointed skywards. 'We're being tailed!'

Ullman spun round, then guffawed. 'A helicopter. Is that all? Seen dozens of 'em lately. It's the oil they're interested in, not us.'

Flying at 1,000 feet, the helicopter stayed well astern of *Scorpion*. Every few minutes, the pilot changed direction – as if surveying the sea for brown stains. But at no time did his attention stray from the bucking boat trailing a streamer of foam.

The pilot flicked a switch and radioed the traffic control room. 'Cruiser under observation. Proceeding west along coast. Approaching Southead. Will continue tracking. Over and out.'

Lieutenant Mitchell stiffened. Surely *Scorpion* wasn't bound for the port . . . the perfect place for a trap. Not wasting a second, he relayed the latest news to police headquarters.

Sirens wailing, three squad cars swept on to the quay at Southead harbour. A big blue van roared after them, closely followed by an ambulance. The procession screeched to a standstill. Doors slammed. Superintendent Compton and John Jenkins hurried from the leading car. Nearby, figures poured out of the vehicles – both uniformed and plain-clothes police. Marksmen, equipped with rifles, leapt from the rear of the van.

Several hundred yards away, Commander Izzard jammed on the brakes and brought his car to a shuddering halt. Unaware of the gathering group further along the quay, he ran towards the Harbour-Master's office.

'Where the hell is he?' Izzard barked down the

telephone. Another officer in the control room explained that Mitchell was busy briefing the police by radio.

'All right, Jones. What news?'

'The cruiser's about a mile from us, sir. Looks like she's coming right into harbour.'

Izzard clenched his fist triumphantly. 'Thanks.'

Meanwhile, on the quay, Superintendent Compton gave the action force instructions. 'The men we're up against are armed and dangerous, part of a ruthless international organization. They, or their associates, have already killed. So expect the worst. Number one priority is to save the children. If blood's shed, it'd better not be theirs . . .'

Compton paused, eyeing the ambulance. Then he outlined his campaign of attack. 'Concealed sharpshooters will be deployed around the dock and on launches. You will keep in touch with me via walkie-talkies. No one is to fire without my permission,' he stressed. 'Understood?'

Final tactics would depend on *Scorpion*'s movements and what happened aboard, Compton concluded.

At that moment, Commander Izzard joined the group. A quick glance told him everything. Nodding to Jenkins and Compton, he said: 'She's on her way in, just entering the estuary. Six miles off. Gives you a bit of time to prepare a reception committee . . .'

Superintendent Compton ordered his men to take up their positions. He turned to Izzard. 'Better alert other vessels in port.'

'That's been done, Superintendent. And Navy launches are recording the cruiser's progress.'

Compton was impressed. With the ghost of a smile, he asked: 'Ever considered becoming a policeman?'

But the superintendent didn't wait for an answer. Suddenly, Izzard and Jenkins found themselves alone on the quay – two frightened parents thinking their private thoughts.

In the see-sawing cabin, Bert fiddled nervously with his gun. 'Stinking job!' he muttered. 'Babysitting a couple of snotty kids. Then we have to risk our necks for that Greek nutter.'

'Quit bellyaching!' growled Ullman. 'We'll soon be rich enough to retire.'

Next door, Gary left Susan's side. He undid the Scout's knife, examining it thoughtfully. Any hope of picking the lock?

Above, in the cockpit, the seaman sighed. Smoother water. 'Thank Gawd!' Slowing the engine, he began to ease *Scorpion* through the estuary . . .

Fifty pairs of eyes kept watch on the advancing cruiser. From the traffic control room, from bobbing boats, from the steep sterns of ships, from warehouse roofs . . . lookouts tracked her course.

Aboard a launch, Superintendent Compton made radio contact with the action force. Marksmen checked their rifle sights, tested the triggers, loaded ammunition.

On the bridge of the survey vessel *Trident*, Izzard and Jenkins strained forward anxiously. A huge clock ticked away in Izzard's imagination. Was *Scorpion* still butting towards the harbour? If so, she should show up any moment now . . .

The captain strode across. 'Just received a severe storm warning. All vessels advised to stay in port until further notice.'

Izzard grunted. Already, hoisted black cones would be rattling against the flag-pole outside Southead traffic control room . . . Dammit! Where's *Scorpion*?

As if replying, the radio squawked. 'Target changing course. Appears to be heading for moored cargo liner . . .'

Jenkins stared at Izzard. 'What's it mean?'

But the radio interrupted. 'Launches converging on target. Estuary mouth being blockaded . . .'

Commander Izzard grinned. 'It means, my friend, that the cruiser's cornered!'

Scorpion's engine idled as she swung into the shadow of the ship's hull. Ullman grabbed the suspended rope ladder. Craning his neck, he saw Mercouri's face far above.

'Come on!' Ullman beckoned.

But the Greek didn't come. Instead, he waved his arms wildly and shouted. Though the words weren't clear, Bert's sharp ears caught one of them . . . 'Trap!'

The weasel swivelled. Boats! Creeping closer like a wolf pack!

Ullman released the ladder. 'Get us out of here!' he bellowed.

In the cockpit, the sailor opened the throttle. The engine snarled. Twin propellers whipped the water.

Wake seething, *Scorpion* began her all-or-nothing race . . .

Superintendent Compton cursed. He'd miscalculated badly. 'After her!' Grimly, he pictured the young hostages. As the flotilla gave chase, Compton raised a loud-hailer and called on *Scorpion* to surrender.

'Never!' Ullman spat from the cruiser's stern. Then, yelling above the engine roar, he told Bert: 'If the cops get too close, bring those brats to me . . .'

In the traffic control room, Lieutenant Mitchell paced to the window. A right mess! he thought. Still, she can't escape. The port's sealed off.

Trident drummed full speed ahead. On the bridge, Jenkins chain-smoked. He glanced sideways – Izzard was chalk-white. No trace now of his earlier confidence. He passed Jenkins the binoculars. 'That cruiser's greased lightning. Nothing can keep up with her.'

Jenkins focused on *Scorpion*'s squat stern, drawing further and further away from the pursuing launches. He returned the binoculars without comment.

Suddenly, Izzard exclaimed. A tug had put out from the dock and was trying to intercept the cruiser . . .

Aboard *Scorpion*, the crewman gulped, wrenched the wheel. Swerving, zig-zagging, the cruiser danced clear of the slower tug. But moments later, a grinding crunch jarred the whole boat. Bert fell heavily. Ullman rushed to the cockpit. 'What the . . .'

'Hit a log,' gasped the sailor. 'Go below, check she's not holed and taking in water.'

Ullman obeyed – this was no time to argue. Soon after, he re-appeared. 'Can't *see* any damage.' The seaman signalled his relief and pushed *Scorpion* back to maximum revs.

Meanwhile, the flotilla had narrowed the gap. But not for long. *Scorpion* was running flat out again. Superintendent Compton glowered. The quarry was just too fast for the pack . . .

Careering onwards, the cruiser neared the mouth of the estuary. 'They'll never catch us!' Ullman shouted contemptuously. He was almost enjoying the chase and the yowling wind wet with stinging spray.

Then something happened, something that wiped the smirk off Ullman's face. The engine started to splutter. It revived, coughed, choked into silence. The sailor hollered: 'I'll try and fix it. Take over the wheel.' He darted away.

Ullman stood helplessly behind the cockpit instruments. He bawled at Bert: 'Get the kids up here where the cops can see 'em. And your gun, too . . .'

Bert plunged downstairs.

But a minute before, Gary had finally managed to pick the cabin door lock. He and Susan were sneaking along the corridor when they heard Bert's pounding feet. Desperately, the children hid in the only place they could think of – the thugs' cabin. Bert's footsteps clattered past, then halted.

Gary held his breath. A loud curse came from next door. Susan trembled. Would the weasel sniff them out? No . . . the sound of running!

In *Scorpion*'s cockpit, the sweating sailor seized the wheel. He pressed a button. The engine growled, purred throatily . . .

Ullman stepped out on deck, colliding with Bert, who blurted: 'Kids gone!' The giant gaped. 'What?'

But they said no more. For, with a sudden shock, both saw that the pursuing pack was snapping at their heels . . .

'Surround her!' Superintendent Compton lowered the walkie-talkie. *Scorpion* . . . stationary . . . only a few yards ahead. The hunt was over!

Compton should have known better than to count his chickens. Abruptly, as though waking, the cruiser shook. In no time, she was charging off again.

From the bridge of *Trident*, Izzard watched unbelievingly. Not because *Scorpion* had eluded capture, but because he had spotted his son. Gary and Susan were stealing across the deck. Now they'd concealed themselves in a dinghy!

Someone else had seen the children's flight – the crewman at *Scorpion's* helm. He ought to tell the others, but . . . Any such thought was banished from his mind by what he noticed next. A line of barges stretched across the estuary mouth!

He yelled to Ullman. 'We can't get out! Must give up.'

The giant lurched into the cockpit. 'Shut up!' he hissed. 'Just steer.'

In the traffic control room, Mitchell groaned. 'They're gonna try to break through the blockade. Crazy. Never make it. And if they do, the storm . . .'

Scorpion ran back and forth along the line of barges, like a trapped animal searching for a hole. There *was* a gap. Too tight? The sailor swallowed, then drove full tilt between two barges. A horrible noise of scraping and splintering. She'll be crushed! The seaman closed his eyes. Five seconds later, he opened them.

Amazing! We've beaten the blockade!

But his joy turned to dread when he caught sight of the waiting waves.

The barges lumbered aside to make way for *Trident* and a trio of tugs. Aghast, John Jenkins stared at the retreating boat which held his only child. He remembered Joan's heart-broken words when she learnt of the kidnap. Was worse to come?

Like monstrous paws, wave after wave smacked and swatted *Scorpion*. The cruiser reeled dizzily – was flung up, down, sideways. Then, as if tiring of its violent game, the sea seemed to give a mighty shrug. *Scorpion* was lifted high . . . and dropped. Immediately, she capsized.

'She's sinking!' Izzard said in a strangled voice. 'Gary . . . Susan!'

A red-white-and-blue lifeboat battered through the besieging water. Hopeless? No! Look! Figures clinging to *Scorpion*'s upturned hull! One, two, three . . . A boy's dark-haired head bobbed to the surface.

Izzard cheered, but the sound stuck in his throat. Gary had gone under again!

Later, shivering in the lifeboat, Gary could hardly recall diving to save Susan. It was a miracle he'd found her, tangled in a rope six feet beneath *Scorpion*. Ullman, Bert and the sailor had been picked up, too. Not that Gary cared. Fighting back the tears, he watched a lifeboatman give artificial respiration. Please don't die, Susan!

CHAPTER FIFTEEN

Round-up

In a hospital ward, John and Joan Jenkins sat silently by a bed. Gary stood on the other side, a package under his arm. All three peered intently at a pale face, framed by blonde hair. Susan's head stirred on the pillow. Her eyelids fluttered. Then she was awake. 'Where . . . Oh, Mum, Dad!'

Mrs Jenkins started crying. Jenkins took his daughter's hand. The girl's gaze wandered . . . and found Gary. '*You're* here, too!' Her voice was faint, but the delight was obvious.

Gary grinned. 'Gave us a real scare, you did!'

Memories flooded into Susan's mind. *Scorpion*! The water!

'He saved your life,' Jenkins said hoarsely. 'We'll never be able to thank him enough.'

Gary quickly changed the subject. 'S'pose you've forgotten what today is, Susan.'

She looked puzzled.

'It's your birthday, idiot. Many happy returns!' Gary handed over the parcel.

Susan carefully undid the colourful wrapping paper. 'A bird book! Just the one I wanted. How did you know?'

Gary winked, then blushed slightly as Susan insisted on kissing him.

She smiled slowly. 'I'm thirteen now, the same age as you. No more bossing me about.'

They both laughed.

Outside Southead Hospital, the streets were thronged with tourists. The holiday season was in full swing. But while visitors enjoyed the oil-free beaches, Superintendent Compton and his men had no time to relax. Around Britain, police forces swooped on Intercon's allies – some of them 'highly-respected' citizens.

'They'll get what they deserve,' Compton told Jenkins later. 'Thanks partly to information reported by your daughter's young friend. Quite a lad, that!'

Jenkins wasn't surprised to learn that Mercouri had 'grassed', betraying Intercon in the hope of avoiding a stiff jail sentence. But he *was* intrigued by part of the Greek's confession. It concerned Duncan Farrar, captain of *Olympus*. Years ago, Mercouri – not his real name – had caused a serious collision at sea. Farrar had witnessed everything and given evidence against the other man, though they never met. As a result, the Greek lost his master's licence. He swore he'd have revenge . . .

So that's why Farrar didn't recognize Mercouri during the *Saracen* trial! Jenkins grinned ruefully. The puzzle was complete.

Abroad, the police also swung into action. Testimonies from Ullman and Bert led to the arrest of Hans, the German knife-thrower who murdered Larsen, as well as Donovan's killers. Across the five continents – Europe, America, Africa, Asia, Australia – law officers tracked down the big and small criminals of Intercon. The job took many months. Among those held for questioning was Schmidt, Dupont's replacement, who'd arrived too late to carry out his mission – disposing of the children. And what of Abdul Hussein, the scheming brain behind it all? He vanished, and detectives are still hunting him. But Intercon's crimes, including the manslaughter of thirteen *Olympus* sailors, were severely punished. In addition, the organization had to pay millions of pounds' compensation for damaging England's south coast.

Meanwhile, Susan spent the rest of her school holidays as the Izzards' guest. Gary taught her to swim and sail. He has become a keen bird-watcher and, to everyone's amazement, he can now coax a few simple tunes from the piano.

A photograph of Gary, Susan and Snuff appeared on the front page of the local newspaper. With it was an article which praised the children's courage, explaining how they'd helped defeat an international plot, how Gary had rescued Susan from drowning, and how a tousled black springer spaniel had earned the right to go into the dining room whenever he wanted.

In London, John Jenkins was summoned one morning to Richard Langley's office. 'You did well, Jenkins. Glad I put you on the case.'

The insurance investigator bit his lip, trying not to explode. Pompous twit! If it hadn't been for me . . .

'Yes, Regal is most grateful,' added Langley. 'Take a week off. Oh, and I'm sure you'll be pleased to hear that I've been promoted.'

Jenkins forced a smile, and muttered his congratulations. Passing a smug-looking Gloria, he left the room.

At home, Joan was furious. '*You're* the one who should've got promotion . . . and a whopping pay rise!'

John Jenkins shrugged. 'Who cares? Susan's safe. Nothing else matters. And from now on, this family's going to have a lot more fun – together.'